THE SILVER DREAM

THE SILVER

DREAM

AN *INTERWORLD* NOVEL

story by

NEIL GAIMAN AND
MICHAEL REAVES

WRITTEN BY MICHAEL REAVES AND MALLORY REAVES

HarperCollins *Children's Books*

First published in the USA by HarperCollins *Publishers Inc* in 2014
First published in Great Britain by HarperCollins *Children's Books* in 2014
HarperCollins *Children's Books* is a division of HarperCollins *Publishers* Ltd,
77-85 Fulham Palace Road, Hammersmith, London, W6 8JB.

The HarperCollins website address is
www.harpercollins.co.uk

1

Copyright © Neil Gaiman and Michael Reaves 2014

ISBN 978-0-00-752345-0

Printed and bound in England by Clays Ltd, St Ives plc

CHARACTER GUIDE

Joey's Team

Joey Harker

J/O HrKr—male, younger cyborg version of Joey.

Jai—male, senior officer. Spiritual, likes big words.

Jakon Haarkanen—female, wolflike.

Jo—female, has white wings, can fly only on magic worlds.

Josef—male, comes from a denser planet. Large and strong.

Other Walkers of Note

Jaya—female, red-gold hair, voice like a siren.

Jenoh—female, catlike. Mischievous.

Jerzy Harhkar—male, quick and birdlike, feathers for hair. Joey's first friend on Base.

Joaquim—male, new Walker.

Joliette—female, vampirelike. Has a friendly rivalry with Jo.

Jorensen—male, senior officer. Good-natured, taciturn.

Teachers and Officers

Jaroux—male, the librarian. Loves knowledge, is friendly and quirky.

Jayarre—male, Culture and Improvisation teacher. Cheerful, charismatic.

J'emi—female, Basic Languages teacher.

Jernan—male, quartermaster. Strict and stingy with equipment.

Jirathe—female, Alchemy teacher. Body made from ectoplasm.

Joeb—male, team leader, senior officer. Laid-back, brotherly attitude.

Jonha—male, officer. From a magic world. Skin like tree bark.

Jorisine—female, officer. From a magic world. Elflike.

Joseph Harker (the Old Man)—male, the leader of InterWorld. Older version of Joey. Stern, has a cybernetic eye.

Josetta—female. The Old Man's assistant. Friendly, well organized, no-nonsense.

Josy—female, officer, has long golden hair with knives braided into it.

CHAPTER ONE

CALL ME JOE.

Please.

It's not that I have anything against "Joey"—it's a perfectly good name, and it's worked fine for the first sixteen years of my life. But that's the point. I'm sixteen now, almost seventeen, and the name "Joey" just doesn't feel like me anymore. Which maybe isn't surprising, given that I've met more versions of myself than *Star Wars* has clones. When you stop to think about it, I've probably got the biggest identity crisis of all time going, so if I want to drop one lousy letter from my name, I think I'm entitled.

I was trying to explain this to Jai, which wasn't easy, considering that we and the rest of the team were pinned down by Binary scouts shooting what looked like elongated blobs of mercury at us, and Jai's not the easiest person to talk to unless you happen to have a dictionary chip installed between your ears. Which I don't.

He listened, returning fire with more mercury blobs (which are called "plasma pods" in case you're wondering), and then asked, "Are you unambiguously certain?" Behind him, Jakon leaped on top of a power condenser, crouching all sleek and furry, snarling as she looked for more prey. The wolf girl version of me looked like she might be enjoying this a little. She always did, but I suppose there was nothing wrong with loving your job. . . .

"Excuse me," Jai said crisply, aiming over my shoulder down the length of the big chamber in the abandoned power plant. He fired the emitter, which made a sort of *thwip!* sound. I caught a crazy, distorted glimpse of movement from behind me, reflected off the chest area of Jai's encounter suit: a Binary scout on a grav-board, trying for a sneak attack. Then the plasma pod hit him and negated the binding force in his atomic nuclei, which is how Jai would've described it. Me, I'd just say he disappeared in a puff of smoke and a sound like *zzzapht!!*

This caused a momentary lull in the fighting on both sides, which I took advantage of to ask what he meant. "Huh?" I said. (I get a lot more mileage out of words than Jai does.)

"Are you unambiguously certain?" he repeated patiently. He pointed the emitter in various directions. *Thwip. Thwip.*

Next to me, J/O fired his laser-cannon arm at a group of

attacking scouts. "That means *are you sure*," he offered help-fully, and I rolled my eyes. J/O *did* have a dictionary chip installed between his ears, and took every opportunity to make me aware of it. I ignored him.

"That I want to change my nickname? Yes."

"No, that your chronological age is in fact sixteen."

I started to tell him that his brain had finally grown too big for his head, but stopped. He had a point.

Though we don't time travel in the classic sense in the InterWorld organization, we all know that time itself isn't independent, aloof, and serene from all the myriad worlds that make up the various versions of Earth. Though I'd never encountered any Earths on which time itself seemed subjectively altered—Earths on which everyone seemed to ta-a-a-l-lk-k . . . r-e-e-a-l . . . s-l-o-o-w . . . or Earths where *everyoneranaroundliketheywereinanoldsilentmovieandtheyalltalked-likethis!*—still, most people knew that time passed quicker or slower in some planes as opposed to others. Just as it was also known that after some time spent in those worlds, your own time sense, not to mention your body, adjusted to the new temporal reality.

I'd been in quite a few such parallel planes in the time I'd been a member of InterWorld. Which meant that Jai had a valid reason for asking, but only up to a point. I might be, as far as I knew, older than my birthday said I was. Or younger. Problem was, there was no way to measure the rate that time passed "outside" the plane we were in. And even if there were, what about time spent in the In-Between, that crazy-quilt collision of various realities and worlds that a Walker used as a shortcut from one reality to the next? Besides, it was all subjective, tied in with consciousness, so really, you only were "as old as you felt."

I said as much to Jai, who looked at me as if I'd just pointed out to him that the sky was blue. (Usually. On this world it was more greenish.) "Indubitably," he said, and then he lost me again. "And are you unquestionably certain your haecceity is defined by your moniker?"

"My *what*?"

"Your moniker. Your name."

"I know that one. My . . . hi-ex-it . . . ?"

"Haecceity. Your *you*ness. The qualities that make you you, rather than me."

"Even I didn't know that one," J/O admitted, looking like he was filing it away somewhere—which he likely was.

"That's an ironic thing to ask," I said, "considering that you *are* me. Or I'm you, whichever."

"Yet we all possess qualities which render us unique. Haecceity is the particular characteristics of those qualities that make you *you*."

Thwip. Thwip. Zzzapht!!

I pondered that as another rutabaga bit the dust. I was getting used to seeing it, which was both a relief and a

14

disturbance, if you know what I mean. The emitter dissolved the atomic bonding, which meant no muss, no fuss. They just went poof—or *zzapht*. And they weren't people in the same sense that we were. They looked human until you got up close; then their skin had a waxy, unfinished look, which made sense, since they were actually clones made primarily from cellulose and plant matter. The Binary was big on cookie-cutter assembly-line cannon fodder, just like HEX's armies of choice were usually zombies. There wasn't much point in feeling bad about killing something that was nine-tenths dead to begin with. But it still bothered me that it was bothering me less, if that makes any sense.

I was about to say something else to Jai, when I heard Josef approaching. Josef came from a world much denser than most of ours, so it wasn't hard to recognize his heavy tread. "What's up, Josef?" I asked, without turning my head. I was tracking another rutabaga.

He didn't reply immediately, so I squeezed off my shot (*thwip!*) and glanced over my shoulder at him. "They've sent in reinforcements," he rumbled, looking troubled.

"How many?" Jai asked, and I knew then it was bad, because Jai usually can't ask anything in less than ten syllables. Josef shook his head.

"Too many to count quickly."

J/O turned and looked at the nearest blank wall. "Tapping into an exterior security cam," he said. J/O's a cyborg version of me, from an Earth that is currently recovering from the Machine Wars. He's got more hydraulic fluid circulating in him than blood, so when I watched the color drain from his face I knew something was *very* wrong. He was younger than me by a few years, and while he always handled himself well on missions—and made sure to point it out when he did—it was moments like this that I was reminded of his youth.

"Let's see," I said.

One of his eyes was cybernetic; it usually looked almost identical to his natural eye, save the circuitry going through it. That eye grew brighter, and on the wall there appeared a black-and-white projection of the outside. At first there was little to see: just more blasted masonry, exposed rebar, and the like. But then—

There was movement.

Lots of movement.

Rutabagas swarmed down the blasted, torn-up streets; over, around, and through walls; and even up from manholes and huge cracks in the pavement. There must've been a hundred in the first couple of minutes. And they just kept coming.

J/O had only tapped into the visual, not the audio, if there even was one. It really was eerie, seeing them coming, wave after wave, in utter silence.

And I realized that the silence also meant the hostilities had stopped inside the power plant. The veggie clones already in here with us had ceased their attack. Of course: No point in wasting more of their numbers when they can just sit back and wait. Six of us against five hundred or so of them . . .

Suddenly my deep and abiding concern over what I wanted to be called didn't seem very important.

The walls and floor began to tremble. They were right outside.

"What now, fearless leader?" This was from Jo, another version of me—a girl with angelic white wings.

"Now I think we die," Josef rumbled. Big guys are usually phlegmatic, and they didn't get much bigger than Josef.

I gripped my emitter hard. "Not on *my* watch," I said.

Jakon looked at me. Her eyes glittered in her furry face. "And what are you gonna do?"

"Think of something," I said, with far more confidence than I felt.

A shot fired by a rutabaga outside demolished the camera J/O was tapped into. The feed dissolved in a burst of static. At the far end of the big chamber I could see what remained of the initial Binary attack force gathering. Behind us a window shattered, and rutabagas began climbing in.

I looked around wildly. Left, right, down, up—there was an air vent above us, the kind that might have led to vent shafts, but I wasn't sure how much help that would be. Certainly Josef couldn't fit up there; he was almost twice my size and about four times as dense. Jo had her wings, but she couldn't do more than glide unless there was enough magic in the air to support flight; this world was completely taken over by Binary, much closer to the technological end of the spectrum than the magical—and she couldn't carry more than one of us anyway.

I raised my arm to give the order to attack. There was no time left and no other choice. I couldn't sense a portal anywhere near us, so we couldn't escape through the In-Between. If Hue had come along on this assignment, things might've been different, but the little pan-dimensional critter's a lot like a cat: Sometimes he just disappears for weeks at a time.

We needed a miracle, but I wasn't going to put a lot of faith in the term "deus ex machina" when we were surrounded by Binary.

We'd have to fight. Before I could give the order, however, the air in front of us began to glow. It was warm, the kind of cozy heat that radiated from a fireplace on a cold night. The glow formed an oval shape, and through it stepped a girl.

My age, no more—if that. She had shaggy black hair and wore a strange outfit that seemed cobbled together out of various locales and times: Moorish pantaloons, a mantle from the Renaissance, a blouse that looked Victorian. I noticed all those later, though. At the moment all I noticed were her hands.

Actually her fingernails, to be exact. Each nail looked

like a tiny circuit board. She pointed her right index finger at the Binary scouts. The nail glowed green, the rutabagas were surrounded by a green light, and . . . froze. Not in terms of temperature but in terms of movement. Then she pointed her left pinkie at us; it glowed, and we were all enveloped in a purple light.

Just before the room disappeared, she looked at me. I had a brief impression of long lashes surrounding violet eyes. "Hey, cutie," she said. And winked.

I saw Jakon give me a big grin, full of fangs. And I knew, as the chamber vanished from around us, that I'd turned crimson clear to the tips of my ears.

CHAPTER TWO

THE IRONY IS THAT I've been known to get lost just going from my bunk to the bathroom.

I used to think it was simply that I had no sense of direction. And it's true—I didn't. But one thing I've learned over the last two years is that things are never simple. It turns out that my lousy sense of direction is limited to the first three spatial dimensions: longitude, latitude, and altitude. But there are other directions, lots of them. Eight at least, and probably a whole bunch more.

If you're like I was at first, just trying to visualize eight or more ways that proceed at right angles on top of the three we already have gives you a massive ice cream headache. Where are these other dimensions? Why can't we interact with them the way we do with the three we already have?

Well, according to the brain trust at Base Town, they were "compactified" (one of the fun things about being a scientist is being able to make up new words) the instant this universe began; somehow they were shrunk down to distances less than the diameter of an atom. If you pick any one of the "big three"—let's say "up"—you can use it as an infinite vector and head away from the Earth—past the moon, past Mars . . . out of the solar system and into the dark. You'll never run out of "up."

That's because we live—most of us, anyway—in a three-space world (or four, if you want to get technical). In a three-space world there's just enough room for three vectors to proceed at ninety degrees from a point; they're mutually perpendicular. (Time is a constant until we get fairly far up the asymptotic curve, so we can ignore it for now.) But there are also universes where the rules are "looser," where there's more "room" for new directions to exist.

I know—it's hard to conceive of such things. But remember: All we really know of the universe is what filters in through our senses, and that isn't a whole lot. Take the electromagnetic spectrum. It includes virtually every ripple of energy that powers the cosmos, from the long, lazy radio waves we communicate with through microwaves that we cook with all the way up to X-rays and gamma rays, which pack enough punch into their wavelengths to outshine an entire galaxy. All that majesty, all that infinite variety of energy, and all we see is a narrow little slice of it: seven measly colors. It's like being invited to a royal banquet and then only being allowed to pick the crumbs off one plate.

So, take everything I just told you, and then try to imagine it all at once. Things moving at angles you didn't even know existed, inverting and reverting and transforming, all painted with colors and textures and noises, and mash it all together. Then picture it reflected in two cracked mirrors, facing each other. That's *kind of* what the In-Between is like.

That's where the girl took us, though it was by far the most wrenching transition I'd ever experienced. I'd traveled to the In-Between more times than I could count by now, and the jump had never once made me feel as queasy as it did when she brought us there.

That's where we were, though; I could tell before I even opened my eyes. All my senses, both internal and external, were verifying it. I could tell by the incredible and ever-changing sounds: mostly wind chimes but occasionally faraway noises like car horns, rumblings, birdsongs, water flowing, and every now and then the strains of an old instrumental from the 1930s that my dad was fond of, "Powerhouse," by Raymond Scott. If you've ever watched an old Warner Bros. Looney Tunes cartoon, you've probably heard it. I could smell paprika; chocolate; and an astringent, medicinal smell that I couldn't identify. The breeze felt now like feathers, now like fine-grain sandpaper. All this before I even opened my eyes.

So I opened my eyes.

I was standing on what looked like a Rand McNally globe

of a terrestrial planet. It was maybe twenty feet in diameter and I was sticking out from it at a forty-five-degree angle, halfway between the equator and the South Pole, just like the Little Prince on his asteroid (assuming the South Pole was on the "bottom" relative to me and the rest of my team, who were standing or floating upon or nearby a whole slew of various other improbabilities).

And something wasn't right.

That probably seems like a pretty ridiculous statement; after all, when is anything ever right about the In-Between? It's the essence of *wrongness*, entropy's landfill. Saying there was something not right about it was like saying there was something a *little* scary about Lord Dogknife.

But the feeling was unmistakable. Furthermore, it wasn't going away.

Jo opened her eyes then, and by the look on her face, I could tell she felt the same way.

J/O looked accusingly at me. "Where did you take us?"

"Hey, *I* didn't take us anywhere! It was that girl," I said. Technically, Jai was our senior officer, but after a training mission had gone awry and I'd rescued them from the clutches of HEX, most of them tended to look to me in a pinch. There are drawbacks to being even an unofficial team leader, the biggest of which is getting blamed for everything.

"Fine, then where'd your *girlfriend* take us?" Jo's voice was as accusing as J/O's glare, and it probably didn't help my case that I was crimson again, but I tried to protest anyway. "She's not my—"

Before I could finish, several members of my team gave little reactions of surprise, looking past me. I whirled as the unfamiliar voice sounded from behind me, my hands coming up in a defensive position. I know it sounds like cheesy kung fu movie stuff, but you learn to think fast in the In-Between.

"Yes, I'd say that *is* rather premature," said the mysterious girl, giving me another wink, "since we've only just met."

"Who *are* you?" The question was clear and strong, the voice of someone not at all intimidated—unfortunately, it was Jakon's voice, not mine. All I'd managed to do was stutter. My tongue felt like it was tied in a Gordian knot.

"A friend," she answered easily, giving a little shrug of one shoulder. When I'd still been home—before my life became cluttered with Multiverses, Altiverses, and versions of me sporting fur, fangs, wings, and bionic implants—I had a wild, passionate, undying crush on a girl named Rowena. Rowena had sometimes done that artless little shrug when she was being silly or coy. I'd come to covet it, to take it as proof that I could amuse her in some way, even if all I'd said to prompt it was "That test was murder, huh?" or "Do they really expect us to run a mile in eight minutes?"

"Not good enough," I said. I stepped off the miniature world and onto a bright red cube the size of a steamer trunk that was busily engaged in turning itself inside out. It stabilized as soon as my shoe touched it. Gravity shifted to accommodate, and behind me the "planet" collapsed into a point and vanished. I hardly noticed. Oddly, the memory of Rowena had strengthened my resolve a bit. I'd never been able to talk to her because, really, what do you say to a girl like that when you're just one guy in a school of hundreds? There had been nothing special about me then.

Now, however, I was more than just a high school kid—I was a Walker. (Although, when you get right down to it, now I was essentially one guy in an army of a few hundred different versions of me, but thinking of it like that wasn't conducive to my self-esteem right then.) "Tell me who you are, where you've taken us, and—"

She looked at me with what might have been something akin to respect but was more likely just surprise that the blushing idiot was able to form sentences. Probably the latter, because instead of actually answering me, she said, "You honestly don't recognize the In-Between?"

"Of course I recognize—" I began, only to have her talk over me again.

"Then that renders your second question a little superfluous, doesn't it?"

I kept talking, going right over her as she finished. "—but it's not *our* In-Between." As I said it, it became clearer to me that whatever was wrong about the In-Between was her doing. She was an unknown, and quite possibly an agent of either HEX or the Binary. But even so, I was inclined to trust her—and that *really* scared me. I couldn't risk her finding out the way back to Base. The notion wasn't likely; it took a specific formula to get back to InterWorld, and only Walkers knew it. She was clearly not a Walker. Yet, she'd traversed the In-Between. . . .

She gave me a considering glance. "You're right. And wrong, but mostly you're right. I'm sorry about that; I needed to make sure the Binary were off your trail." She gave that same one-shouldered shrug and a wink. "Not to worry; it's fixed."

Then that purple light enveloped us again, before we could react, and that same sense of severe dislocation, worse than anything I'd ever experienced before—

And then we were home, back on the base that we all recognized. Everything was as it should be. We'd made it back to InterWorld.

Only . . .

She was with us.

CHAPTER THREE

THE OLD MAN IS . . .

If your principal and your sternest grandparent had a child born on the last day of summer before school starts, and that child grows up in the moment you realize you've been caught filching a cookie from the jar. In other words, he exists simply to remind you of all the bad things you've ever done, all the things you've ever failed at, and all the mistakes you will ever make.

At least, that's what it feels like. Especially when you've failed a mission.

Which we had. We all stood there in his office, hardly daring to breathe as he looked at each of us in turn. Even the new girl was silent.

"I don't think I have to tell you again how important this mission was, or how miserably you botched it."

His bionic eye glittered accusingly as he talked. No one's

ever figured out what that eye is made of—some say it's a Binary construct, some say it's a regular glass eye magicked by HEX—but we all pretty much agree it could see into our souls.

Part of the reason I find it so unnerving to be run through the ringer by the Old Man is that, out of everyone at Base Camp (including J/O), the Old Man looks the most like me. Except he looks like me in a few decades, a few wars, a handful of personal tragedies, and a couple of reconstructive surgeries. He's like your conscience personified; he knows you could have done better, because he pretty much *is* you.

He also has room in his cranium for amounts of data that seem to be bigger than the combined memory clouds of all the computers on any thousand different Earths.

"I sent you to Earth FΔ98^6 for a very specific reason, and you returned in less than an hour, empty-handed save an unauthorized visitor."

I opened my mouth—why, I wasn't sure. I still didn't even know her name, so it's not like I could introduce her.

Luckily, I didn't have to worry about it.

"Acacia Jones," she said confidently, though she didn't offer her hand to the Old Man. "And *don't*," she said, before I or anyone could do any more than blink. "*Ever.*"

She was looking at me, so I don't think my response was overly paranoid. "Don't *what?*"

"Don't call me 'Casey,'" she said, although her devil-may-care attitude was a mite tempered in the presence of the Old Man. He could ruffle the smoothest of feathers, and his look of tolerant amusement caused her to amend her statement with "Uh, sir. Please."

He assured her, in the most acidic way possible (to my ears, anyway), that he never would, and then ignored her while we gave our report. Though he didn't move, and in fact hardly seemed to even be breathing, his glare grew more and more intense as we told our story.

The silence hung heavy in the air for a few moments after we finished, and we knew enough not to break it. At least, most of us.

"I'm sorry, sir, but it would have wound up the same way, regardless."

"I'll thank you to keep your mouth shut, young lady, and your nose where it belongs." The Old Man turned his glare on our stowaway, who straightened up slightly under the force of it.

"I *am* sorry, sir. But—"

Sitting there quietly, not moving or raising his voice, the Old Man nevertheless managed to give the impression that a bomb had gone off inside his cramped and cluttered office. Out of the corner of my eye I actually saw several of my colleagues flinch, as if seeking shelter from the incoming shrapnel. "Sorry about *what*, Ms. Acacia 'don't-call-me-Casey-on-pain-of-retribution-too-horrible-to-be-contemplated' Jones?"

Acacia drew herself up slightly under the Old Man's eye, taking a breath. I expected her to start talking, but she didn't. She just looked at him, visibly keeping hold of her nerves. After a moment the Old Man said, "Walker, you and your team are dismissed to showers and mess." He sounded bored. He shuffled some papers on his desk, pretending not to notice as we exchanged a glance and stood there for a moment before we headed for the door, including Acacia.

She didn't get far. "*You* are not on his team, Ms. Jones. Sit."

I caught a glimpse of her face, full of equal parts surprise and trepidation, as she started to sit. Then the door closed behind Jai, who was the last to leave the office.

"Did you see that?" J/O whispered once we were safely down the corridor. "She stood up to him. And *won*."

"I believe that may be an exaggeration of the events that transpired," murmured Jai. "Though it was certainly disconcerting and unprecedented."

"And weird," Josef added.

Jai nodded. "Oh, yeah. *Definitely* weird."

There's nothing like a shower and food after going out on a mission. The In-Between somehow makes you feel grimy, like all those sights and sounds and sensations and smells have stuck to you, like you've been rolling around in a preschool art class's trash can. And plane travel is always disorienting on the stomach, so it's usually better if you haven't eaten a lot beforehand. Yep, there's nothing better than a hot shower followed by some hot food, especially if you're able to revel in the congratulations of a job well done.

Which we weren't, this time. But the shower and food were still good, and we were also the most popular table in the mess, since word had gotten around to *everyone* that we'd brought someone back from a mission.

Someone who wasn't one of us.

And the fact that my *entire team* was now referring to the first non-redheaded J-named real person to have appeared on the base in—oh, ever—as my *girlfriend* was making me both very popular and very *not*.

Now, it's not that InterWorld relationships are forbidden, really. It's just that they're not *done*. Why, you ask?

Because it's *weird*.

We're all from different planets and dimensions and realities, sure. But we're also all just similar enough that it would be like hooking up with your first cousin. Whom you've known all your life. Who looks so much like you it's impossible to pretend you're not related.

Besides, we're busy. We've got places to go, worlds to save, first cousins to recruit. Those of us who may have been interested in romance of some kind just don't have time to worry about it.

But this new girl . . .

"She's really not one of us?" someone asked for the ump-teenth time, talking over someone else asking where she was from. The questions were flying like laser beams or fire-tipped arrows or plasma pods, and a dishearteningly large proportion were aimed at me.

"Why'd you bring her here?"

"Where'd you find her?"

"How old is she?"

"Where's she from?" The questions were endless, and I couldn't answer any of them—except one.

"Is she really Joey's girlfriend?"

"No!" I said finally, loud enough to be heard over all the questions. My volume earned a temporary reprieve from the chatter long enough for me to add, "She's *not* my girlfriend, I don't even *know* her."

"Yet," Jo offered smugly, which set off a round of laughter loud enough to wake the Binary, if it ever slept in the first place. My cheeks were burning like those of a squirrel hoarding jalapeños, and I busied myself with my vitamin-enhanced protein cake as though it were real dessert.

My team was enjoying this *far* too much.

The questions continued. Things like "Can we meet her?" and "How long is she staying?" and "Why is she here?" as well as a hundred other ones we couldn't answer and maybe two or three we actually could. I let my team answer those, intervening only when I heard the *g*-word and my name (which was apparently still "Joey," incidentally) in the same sentence, and finished my "dessert." It was only just past lunch, but I was thinking I might have been ready for a nap. I'd been up since dawn on a world with two suns, and it had been a tiring day.

I made my way to my quarters, discovering upon the way that, despite how it had seemed, not everyone on Base had been crowded around our table. There were a few stragglers in the hallways and, after answering several more questions with "I don't know" and "She's not my girlfriend," I took to peering around corners before I actually turned them.

The theme from *Mission: Impossible* kept playing in the back of my mind.

It took me twice as long to get to my quarters that way, but at least I avoided any more questions.

Hue met me at the door, changing from a kind of warning red to a confused beige and back again as I entered. My little mudluff friend—that's MDLF, or multidimensional lifeform for those not in the know—spent most of his time in the In-Between but occasionally liked to come find me on Base. After scaring a few of the newer locals and almost getting fragged a few times, he tended to keep to my quarters, venturing out only when I was with him.

"What is it, Hue?" I asked tiredly. I was ready for that nap. "Did Timmy fall down the well again?"

"You named him 'Hue'? That's adorable. But who's Timmy?"

I didn't even bother to turn. Hue had made himself metallic, affording me a distorted view of my own reflection and that of Acacia Jones sitting behind me in my reading chair, one of my books open in her lap.

I sighed. Would this day *never* end?

INTERLOG

From Acacia's Journal

Really, there are some advantages to being me.

I got to Earth FΔ98⁶ with perfect timing, of course. Okay, I admit it; I like to make an entrance. There's nothing wrong with having a bit of flair now and then, no matter what my brother says. Besides, a timely rescue from certain death tends to get people to trust you—at least, usually. Joseph Harker is proving to be a little more difficult than most of my clients.

I mean, I get that he hasn't had it easy. I've done the full research; I know he got a rough start at the InterWorld academy, what with his handler getting killed. That whole thing was glossed over a bit in the archives, but I can read between the lines; he Walked by accident the first time, like most of them do. Unfortunately for him, Binary and HEX were having it out on a neighboring world, so both of them caught it when he ripped through the dimensions. The Walkers may not be able to do much in stopping the war, but every little bit helps— and their powers are still useful enough to the baddies that they'll snatch up a Walker whenever they can.

There's a footnote in his file that says he's one of the more powerful Walkers we've seen in a while; apparently someone here gave InterWorld a heads-up, and they sent a field officer named Jay after him. Jay got him through the In-Between and a little closer to Base, though not without some snags; that's where the log gets a little muddy. I guess he got nabbed by HEX and Jay had to recover him. He was a good officer, that one; his death really upset a lot of people on InterWorld. I take back what I said about Joseph Harker not having an easy start—that's kind of an understatement. Not that I can really be sympathetic. I can't even let him know he has a file with us, let alone that I've read it. . . .

He really stepped up his training, though; wanted to prove himself, I guess. I can't really blame him—I know I was chomping at the bit to get my sea legs when I was old enough to go for my first voyage. I never got captured by a Tech, though, the way he and his team did by HEX.

That part was pretty well documented. I don't know if we had an Agent there, or if we just did interviews; Agents are more reliable than firsthand accounts, but there weren't any records of one being deployed in the travel log.

Anyway. To the best of my knowledge—which is extensive, believe me—he's the only Walker to have ever been booted from InterWorld. Sent him all the way back home, just because he was the only one to make it back to Base with the full story of how his team got captured. They take no chances on that boat, and if you do anything to raise suspicion even once, your name may as well be Jonah. Escaping from a trap your entire team got caught in is kind of a big deal, no matter what the truth is.

Not that it was his fault, though. That little MDLF of his saved him—and a good thing, too, since I'm pretty sure it's also the reason he got his memories back. I don't know exactly how InterWorld does those brain wipes, but I've seen them done before. They last. His didn't, and it was because his MDLF friend came to find him after he'd had his memory wiped of anything related to InterWorld. After that, he remembered he could Walk and single-handedly rescued his team from HEX. I was pretty impressed to read that part, I'll admit.

That MDLF, though . . . The story kind of makes me want to befriend it, too; who knows how useful it could be? There's almost nothing about it in the archives—then again, not a whole lot is known about multidimensional life-forms in general. They're dangerous, but we have more important things to worry about. Which is why I'm even sitting here in the first place.

I've already read through Joe Harker's entire file—at least, the part that's not classified. Yeah, it miffs me a bit that there's something in his file that's classified. I mean, come on; I may be young for an Agent, but I've got high clearance, and the guy isn't exactly upper deck material. Besides, I volunteered for this job; it'd be nice to know what to expect. I'm sailing blind almost as much as he is, not that I'm gonna let him know that. Heh . . . I have to pretend I don't know anything about his past, which I do, and make him believe I know all about his future—which I don't. I'm sailing into a storm, here.

Joseph Harker, the anomaly of InterWorld. I gotta admit: Even though he's a grouch with a lot to prove, I kinda like him.

CHAPTER FOUR

IT'S DIFFICULT, IN SITUATIONS like these, to determine which question will be the least stupid. I could go with the obvious "How did you get in here?" which would likely just make her laugh, or the equally obvious "What are you doing here?" to which she would probably, judging by past history, snap back a witty one-liner that would leave me with at least two omelets' worth of egg on my face. So I chose to go for the unexpected. Instead of asking a question that would put me at a disadvantage, I could criticize her lack of cultural knowledge and, with luck, make myself feel more confident in the process.

"What, you've never heard of *Lassie*?"

They have all sorts of sayings about the best-laid plans. . . .

"Oh, yeah. The 1950's Earth television series about the collie."

So much for making myself feel more confident. All I'd

known was that there'd been a show called *Lassie* about a smart dog. "You, um, obviously know about the show."

She gave an amused smile and that little shrug. "Yes," she said, in the tone of voice that meant *obviously*. "It ran as a TV series on Earths $K\Omega 35^2$ through $\Omega 76$."

"Right. Of course," I mumbled. "I've just—"

"Not to mention $T\Delta 12$ through 18, where various episodes were reality and not—"

"*I've just* been living with a bunch of people who don't know about *anything* from my world. And sometimes . . ."

"You wish you had someone who could talk about the things you like."

The way she'd said it was like she *knew* it was true. Like she'd pulled it right out of my brain. Or out of my journal, which is where I'd written down that exact phrase a few months ago.

Which also happened to be the very same book she had open in her lap.

She saw me look at it, and made no attempt to pretend she hadn't been reading it. I knew she was waiting for a response, but all I could say was "You're reading my journal" in an "of course" tone of voice.

Her smile wasn't quite so cocksure this time. "You're not mad?"

"No." I hoped I was managing to control the blush I felt roaring like a brush fire up my neck. "It's not like it's a *diary*.

Everyone here is required to keep a log of their activities and their feelings."

She looked relieved, tried to hide it. "I know that. That's why I knew you wouldn't be mad."

Somewhat to my surprise, I realized I wasn't mad, just resigned. "How do you know so much about . . . everything?"

She laughed and closed the journal, leaving it on the chair as she stood, folded her arms, and tossed her hair back. "I had a *great* education. Not to mention long-term memory holographic optimization. How about you? Wanna show me what they teach you here?"

"Not really," I answered automatically, then fumbled as she raised both eyebrows. "Well, yes, sort of, but—"

"Don't worry about clearance. They can't keep me out anyway, and I'm no threat to you. Unless you give me reason to be," she amended, smiling in a way that reminded me of Jakon at her most feral. Jai calls it her "Cheshire wolf" look.

"The Old Man said you could stay?" I hedged.

"Yep. As long as I'm escorted at all times."

"You were in here alone," I told her, then stumbled forward a bit as Hue bumped me from behind. I'd almost forgotten about him. I looked over my shoulder, noting the mudluff was a rather indignant shade of purple. "Sorry, Hue."

He turned a more pleased shade of pink, and Acacia laughed. "He stayed between me and the door the whole

40

time," she informed me—and then linked her arm through mine. "So. Let's have the tour."

I knew that if I walked out there with Acacia on my arm, I would *really* never hear the end of it. Ever. For eternity, squared and cubed. I wasn't remotely ready for that. So I walked her to the door, then used the pretense of opening it as a way to disentangle us. I gestured her through in what I hoped was a gentlemanly fashion.

She gave me a little curtsy before stepping out, her amusement as visible as if she could turn colors like Hue. Praying that everyone I knew—which was pretty much everyone, period—was in class or on assignment, I started down the corridor, mysterious girl on one side and mudluff on the other.

"So where are we now?" She was looking around like we were at a theme park, taking everything in. "Everything" being, at the moment, a corridor with occasional floor-to-ceiling pipes, stanchions, and wallcom panels.

"A corridor. Deck twelve, to be exact."

"I can see that, thanks. In what sector?"

I wasn't sure why I was giving her a tour in the first place, since she'd already known where my room was and knew that the different areas of the ship were specifically called "sectors" (and something about the way she'd said "sector" tugged at my memory in an odd way, like trying to remember a dream you'd had the day before), but it seemed to be making her happy.

"It's the barracks. Sorry, we don't have a fancy name for it or anything."

"Yet," she amended, but I got the feeling she was just saying it to mess with me. It was probably always called the barracks. Why would we want to call it anything else? It wasn't even divided by gender; wasn't much point, especially since there were a few para-incarnations of us who seemed to be both, or neither. As I'd observed before, Acacia was the first real, genuine *girl* who wasn't an incarnation of us.

"So what are you going to show me first?"

"What do you want to see?" I asked, without much hope of a real answer. I didn't get one.

"Whatever you want to show me."

I gave up. I was stuck with her because she'd deemed it to be so, and there didn't seem to be much I could do about it. I wasn't even sure I minded; she was a mystery, and she was interesting, and my complete inability to answer any questions about her had rankled a little. Earlier in the mess hall was probably the most popular I'd ever been in InterWorld, and I hadn't even been able to enjoy it.

"Okay," I said, turning the opposite direction down the hallway that led to the mess hall. That's where pretty much everyone would be right now, and if I had to play tour guide, I'd prefer to do it without an audience. "Well, right next to the barracks are the lockers, where we suit up to go on missions. No one's going out right now, so it should be empty."

"A row of lockers," she commented, looking like she might be making an effort to seem impressed. A considerable effort.

I moved her through the room to the wide double doors nestled between the security pillars. They lit up when we reached them, little red lines scanning over me, then Acacia. I realized I'd better identify her before it decided she was an unknown and therefore dangerous.

"Joe Harker, with—"

"Welcome, Joey." It was the kind of voice that could drive you crazy over the phone, the voice of a maddeningly calm mature female whom you just *knew* was smirking at you, even though she was just a disembodied vocal pattern. "Welcome, Acacia. Proceed."

I turned to glance at her as the doors slid open. Her smirk matched the one I was pretty sure the voice had sported. I had to ask, even though I didn't think she'd give a straight answer. "How'd it know you?"

"I told you. I have clearance." She stepped through the doors into the briefing room, leaving me to hurry after her.

That happened twice more as I showed her the briefing room and the receiving room. I realized as we were walking that, although Acacia had found both the base and my room by herself, she was honestly letting me lead her. I'd taken extensive classes on body language and facial expressions, and I was fairly confident that she truly didn't know her way around. I was just as confident that she'd probably give me a run for my money in a sparring session. She had an economy of movement to her that suggested she was well schooled in some kind of martial art, a liquid grace that was just about as dangerous as it was fascinating.

"So this is where new recruits come in?" She was leaning over the railing, staring out at the world on the other side of the dome. It was kind of hard to tell where the world ended and Base Town started, since the dome was translucent and the floor of the receiving room was covered in perfectly manicured grass.

"Usually, unless there's some problem." I hesitated before explaining further, then continued. If the Old Man had given her prime clearance, he obviously wasn't keeping many secrets. "The formula we all learn is like a generic address; it'll take us to whatever world the base is on, then we blip the radar and the pilots bring InterWorld to us. In a bad situation, the 'port team will teleport people directly into Base—usually to the infirmary—but most of the time the whole ship pulls up and they walk on board."

"Must be a sight to see," she murmured, tilting her head to look up at the sky. It was just growing dark outside.

"It is," I said, remembering where I'd been when the dome picked me up. I remembered Jay's body beside me, and how I hadn't been able to feel anything at all by the time they'd come to get us. "C'mon," I said, my voice a little more gruff than I'd intended it. "I want to show you something else."

There were very few things on InterWorld that weren't run with military precision. We had gardens, libraries, gymnasiums, and even an entertainment room for our downtime, but all were kept neat and clean and overseen by a teacher or senior staff appointed by the Old Man. There was no graffiti on Base Town, no litter, no gum under the desks we studied at. There were no murals, no bushes cut into the shape of dinosaurs, no sculptures—there was nowhere on the entire base that showed we were *people*, with thoughts and feelings and imagination.

Except for the Wall.

Acacia took a few steps into the hall between the receiving room and the infirmary, her expression going from curiosity to genuine, unfeigned awe. "What is this?"

"We call it the Wall. Inventive, I know. It's been around for as long as anyone here, at least. No one remembers who started it. But it's pretty much all we have of those who've fallen."

Acacia reached out carefully, brushing her fingers over a photo: yet another boy who looked like me, except his eyes were silver. I'd never known why. She walked down the length of the hall, looking at everything—or, as much of it as she could. It was impossible to take in *everything*. There were hundreds of pictures, both holo and flat, plus scraps of paper, with appreciations and epilogues scrawled on them.

There were printed epigraphs, as well as words and images painted on the Wall's surface. In one place was the perfectly shed skin of a snake. There were feathers, bits of material, clothing, jewelry, and seashells, along with things I'd never been able to identify because they'd come from worlds I'd never heard of. Some of the holos moved; others were static. Everything that had ever meant something to someone lost on a mission had a place on the Wall.

"This is beautiful," Acacia said finally, and I could tell she truly meant it. Her quirky smile had been replaced with a calm, sad curl of her lips.

"Yeah," I said, looking at my own offering. It had taken a lot of courage to finally put something up here when I'd first arrived. Everyone was giving me hell over Jay's death, and they'd already started a little monument to him on the Wall. He'd been important to a lot of people; his was one of the largest sections. Someone had tacked up a picture of him, someone else, a sketch. There was a funny little drawing on one of the mess hall napkins that was apparently an inside joke, and a book with a note that said *thank you*.

That was most common on Jay's part of the Wall—the thank-yous. In different handwritings, different languages, different colors and ways. They were all taped or projected or drawn around Jay's photo. Mine was one of them, made from the rocks and pebbles of the world where he'd drawn his last breath.

Acacia caught me looking, and turned her attention to the portrait of Jay. "Who was he?"

Though I'd expected the question the moment we stopped at his picture, I still had to take a breath before I could answer. "Jay. He saved my life," I said shortly. "And I got him killed." It's funny how one's need to impress someone is completely forgotten in the face of honest emotion.

"Did you mean to?"

I turned to look at her, aghast. "No!"

"Then don't blame yourself," she said, not looking at me. "If he was protecting you, he knew what might happen."

"He died because I didn't listen to him," I said, trying to keep from snapping, but it was hard. "I ran off to help a mudluff, even though he told me it was dangerous."

"You mean Hue?" She asked. I nodded.

"He was stuck. . . . I didn't know what he was, but he looked scared. Turns out, he *was* scared—he'd been trapped by a gyradon." After Jay's death, I'd done some research and found out exactly what the thing had been that had attacked us. It hadn't made me feel any better, but at least I'd felt a little less like a dumb kid who didn't even know what happened well enough to explain it to anyone.

Acacia nodded, apparently recognizing what kind of monster it had been. "You were right, though. And you saved Hue."

"Yeah," I said, looking back at the Wall. Jay for Hue. Was

that a fair trade? Hue had saved me from getting caught by HEX once, and in turn enabled me to save my team. . . . But maybe if Jay hadn't died, everything would have gone differently. Maybe we wouldn't have been trapped by HEX in the first place, wouldn't have needed saving . . .

It was enough to give me a headache. I looked at Jay's portrait, silent, until Acacia spoke again.

"How many of them did you know?"

"Just him," I said with difficulty. The admission made me feel guilty, like I didn't deserve to be standing in front of all this loss, untouched. *Survivor's guilt*, they call it. Knowing the name of it didn't make it any easier to live with.

"You'll know more," she said. "Eventually."

Oddly, the comment didn't irritate me. She wasn't trying to be smug, or show that she knew more than I did. I knew it was true. You don't fight a war without expecting casualties, and as much as I'd work to not let it happen, I knew more of us would wind up as memories on the Wall. Probably even me.

"Yeah," I said. "I know."

She took my hand.

I showed her the port room—there was some debate over whether or not it was called that because you could teleport to other parts of Base Town from it, or because it was on the far left side of the ship—and looped back around through the second row of lockers to show her the mini theater and the arcades, then took her through the library back to the class-rooms. Most of the classes were done for the day, but a few of my teachers were still coming and going.

I got us out onto one of the higher decks in time for her to witness another phase transition. One of InterWorld's more insidious features was its ability to move both forward and backward in time, spanning a period of more than 100,000 years. And just to make things harder for HEX and the Binary to track us, the soliton array engines were also programmed to go "sideways" in time as well; in other words, they could cross the Dirac walls from one parallel Earth to another. The number of altiversal worlds we crossed to, and the time we stayed in each one, was determined by spells based on quan-tum randomization; there was absolutely no way to break the code pattern.

For the last two weeks we'd had the wards on maximum and the air filters going full blast, because this particular Earth was celebrating its particular anniversary (if that's the word) of the K-T extinction event, which had pretty much wiped out Barney the dinosaur and all his extended family. Only now was the raw, bloody sunlight beginning to break through the global cloud cover, and what it showed wasn't pretty: a scorched Earth, carpeted with the charcoal of what had once been a magnificent old-growth forest.

"Your ship can time travel?" she asked, after I'd explained

what the phase shift was. She seemed incredibly interested, and I was a little too grateful that she was finally asking me a question I could answer.

"Yes and no," I said, trying to give her the same kind of non-answer she always gave me. It didn't exactly work. She just looked at me, and the expectant way she raised her eyebrows made me elaborate further. "We're traveling on a randomly set path, on parallel dimensions of the same three worlds. The ship goes backward and forward, but—"

"But it can't anchor at will," she said authoritatively, giving a knowing nod. "You phase to destinations set by a random variable on those three worlds, but you're still anchored to the alphastream."

I didn't have any clue what she was talking about, but that was more or less par for the course at this point. She seemed satisfied at my nod; what she'd said sounded right, anyway, and I knew we never time traveled beyond going back and forth on our base worlds. I turned to lead her out of the upper deck, down to the class halls. The windows around us were still coated with a thick layer of dust and ash.

"Hey, Jayarre," I said as we passed through one of the open doors. Unlike the school I was used to, we never called teachers by their last names and "Mr." or "Ms."—after all, some of them didn't even have last names.

Jayarre focused on me—I thought he'd been looking at me anyway, which was why I'd said hello, but it was hard to tell with the monocle—and gave a cheerful smile accompanied by an exuberant wave. Jayarre was the Culture and Improvisation teacher. He hailed from an Earth more toward the magic side of things, where he'd once explained that all the world was, literally, a stage. I didn't really understand it beyond that, but he had the look of a circus ringmaster and the disposition of your favorite uncle. "Hello, hello! Showing the lady around, are we?"

He also, like most of the other teachers, often seemed to just *know* things.

"Yeah," I said, pausing in the doorway. "This is Acacia Jones."

"Well met, my dear, well met!" He rose and crossed the room in three giant steps to shake her hand. She didn't seem at all rattled. "Are you enjoying your tour *du jour*, madame?"

"*Vachement, monsieur!*" she responded, which I recognized from Basic Language Studies as an emphatic agreement.

Jayarre's eyebrows rose almost to the brim of his top hat, mustache lifting with his grin. "*Merveilleuse, ma bichette!*"

"I was going to show her the Hazard Zone," I interrupted, only to have those eyebrows turned toward me next.

"Were you, now? Well, why not, why not? If she has prime clearance, I see no way at all in which this could go even remotely wrong!" Jayarre was kind of like Jai sometimes, except that instead of using words with lots of syllables, he just used a lot of words. "Perhaps I shall join you on your wondrous journey!"

I hadn't anticipated that, but before I could come up with any possible reason he shouldn't, someone else passed by the door.

"Office. Meeting," she said shortly, turning to glance at me. Jirathe was the Alchemy teacher, and never used two words if one would do. She looked as human as me, save the minor quibble that her cells were made from ectoplasm instead of protoplasm. As a result, her body was sort of a uniform translucent gray when she wasn't moving. But when she was . . . well, the human body is made of more than six trillion cells, each one mostly water. Whenever Jirathe moved, it was like six trillion prisms catching whatever light there was. Or, to put it another way, it was like a rainbow exploding.

"Should I head back to the briefing room?" I hadn't heard anything over the speakers, but maybe something important was happening.

"No." Jirathe gave Jayarre a significant glance, then continued down the deck, through a shaft of crimson sunlight that made her bare arms and shoulders ripple like a fireworks display.

Jayarre murmured, "Sorry about that, my boy. Sounds like senior staff only." He turned back to Acacia, taking her hand and pressing a kiss to her knuckles. "Lovely to meet you, my dear. Perhaps we can exchange pleasantries another time, but now I've got to dash. *À bientôt*."

"*Enchanté!*" Acacia called over her shoulder as we parted ways, and I noticed several of the other teachers filing out of their classrooms and heading in the direction of the Old Man's office. What was the meeting about? Acacia, probably. Was he going to revoke her clearance? No, he'd have no reason to. . . . He wouldn't have given it to her in the first place if he didn't trust her.

"It's about me, I bet," she said cheerfully. If she was sharing any of the same thoughts as I, she seemed completely at peace with them.

"Probably. That doesn't bother you?"

"It'd bother me if they *weren't* having a meeting," she said, and I paused to glance at her. "You're fighting a war here, and you've suddenly got a stowaway on your boat. Wouldn't you call a meeting to make sure everyone knew about a potential threat?"

"The Old Man didn't think you were a threat."

She tilted her head at me. "You sure? He gave me clearance, but do you really think he's not making sure everyone knows it, just in case?"

I thought about that for a moment, going over what she'd said and the way she'd said it. "Are you?"

"Am I what?"

"A potential threat."

"You're a Walker, aren't you? You move between dimensions. You know that 'potential' is a heavy word."

I couldn't help it; I smiled, just a little. "True. So you *are* a potential threat."

"Sure I am," she said, looking at me seriously. Her eyes, as I noticed before, were unmistakably violet, not that she looked anything other than human. Aside from her circuit-board nails, that is. "Or I'm an ally. You think that's only up to me?"

Behind us, reality shimmered, twisted, and re-formed into a completely different, though no less extreme, environment. I tore my gaze from Acacia's to find that we were hovering over an equatorial glacier. Welcome to Snowball Earth, where for millions of years even the oceans were frozen solid. I glanced back at Acacia to see if she'd noticed the small time jump. She was looking out the window as well, with an odd, peaceful smile.

"No," I said in response to her last statement, and she smiled at me. The heating elements kicked in as I turned toward the physical training section of the ship, but I was pretty sure that smile could have warmed me up by itself.

CHAPTER FIVE

THE HAZARD ZONE IS like the best virtual reality game ever, except that on occasion—or even most of the time, really—it will try to kill you. It's the Holodeck and the Danger Room combined, with five stages of different variables and conditioning. It's not that stage 1 is entirely harmless and stage 5 is real danger—the different levels merely indicate how *badly* things will hurt you. Some of the challenges are real, some of them are illusory, and all of them are programmed with random or hidden variables: A rock appears under your foot as you're trying to dodge a series of spears, or a swarm of hornets is stirred up by the particle blast you've just diverted into a tree.

Getting hurt in the Hazard Zone is like a rite of passage. Everyone does it at least once. You're not really one of us until you've been sent to the infirmary with a third-degree burn because there was the tiniest bit of doubt in your mind that the fire-breathing salamander that just leaped out of the cave could really hurt you.

You learn fast. I did.

My first Hazard Zone injury was better than some (J/O had broken a servo when part of the ground had actually caved under his weight) and worse than others (Jerzy Harhkar's only injury had literally been a paper cut during an "attack on the school" scenario). I'd stumbled onto a spinedog variable while training in a jungle simulation. If you've never met a spinedog, don't feel bad; I hadn't, either. It seemed likely that they had those spines for a reason, and that they knew how to use them—what I hadn't known was that part of the reason (aside from the obvious) that they were called spinedogs was their choice of habitat. Not wanting to disturb their nest, I'd ducked around the nearest tree, putting a hand on the bark to steady myself—

—and nearly jumped out of my skin as the *tree* swelled up like a puffer fish. Hundreds of tiny, wooden needles stabbed into my palm, and not only had I stumbled back into the path of the simulated HEX agent I'd been playing cat and mouse with, I failed the sim because I couldn't draw my blaster with my arm numb to the elbow.

It was hardly the most painful thing I'd ever experienced, but having those needles removed was no fun at all, and using my hand was difficult for two weeks afterward. It hadn't even left me with any cool scars to show off.

Acacia was looking at the empty room with the kind of interested skepticism we all start out with, but I really didn't want to drag her to the infirmary after her first session. "It doesn't seem very big," she commented finally, crossing from one wall to the next in about twenty-five big steps.

"Not until you're running for your life from a cyborg velociraptor, no. The floor is made of anisotropic treadmills that move with you when you run. The scenery moves around you. Makes it feel pretty real, once you get over the fear that it's gonna malfunction and send you smack into a wall."

Acacia giggled. "Has that ever happened?"

"Not that I know of, but I'm always afraid it will."

"I would be, too." She paused. "Can we . . . ?"

I hated having to tell her no. I wasn't sure why, but I did. "Nah. Only a few people have the codes, and they're all . . . not here. Right now." I was also hesitant to remind her of the meeting—which was most likely about her—going on upstairs, even though she hadn't seemed particularly concerned. I just wanted her to feel welcome . . . after all, she might be staying. "Probably tomorrow, though. People use it all the time, and you're a guest, so I'm sure we could fit you in."

"That's okay. Is there a kitchen around here? I'm starving."

"Yes," I hedged a little. Kitchen meant mess hall, and mess hall meant people, and people meant awkward. At least in this situation. "But it'll probably be pretty full . . ."

"I don't mind. Which way?" She smiled cheerfully at me,

and I felt my heart and stomach collide. I was pretty nervous about having to introduce her to everyone who'd been calling her my girlfriend.

"Uh, back the way we came." I turned to go, offering a hand to Hue as he met us at the door. Hue didn't like the Hazard Zone. He'd popped in to see me once in the middle of a simulation, and I thought he was going to have a coronary—if mudluffs even have hearts. He'd turned a confused grayish, then a few different shades of red or pink, all of which seemed to mean *alarmed*, then he'd basically turned into a multicolored disco ball. If anyone in the room had been prone to seizures, Hue would have done them in right then. Then he'd vanished, and I hadn't seen him for almost a whole week. To tell the truth, I'd been getting worried by the time he finally showed up again.

I'd tried to ask him about it, but hadn't gotten much of a response. He seemed confused any time I'd brought it up. The one time I'd been sort of "linked" with him, I'd gotten an impression of the In-Between making perfect sense, from his point of view. I suspected that, for Hue, being in the Hazard Zone was like how my mom used to get sick on virtual reality rides at theme parks; she'd say that because her body wasn't doing what the world around her was telling her it was doing, it caused a weird dislocation. I guess being a multidimensional life-form in a room full of 3-D special effects and things that weren't actually what they looked like must have been a little bizarre.

Walking through the halls with a girl on one side and a mudluff on the other was, as I'd mentioned before, a little weird. I mean, I knew I was the odd one out as far as many things went—and let me tell you how much fun it was living with a bunch of people who are as similar to you as people could get and *still* being the odd one out—but this only served to reinforce it. I was the one who'd gotten Jay killed. I was the one who'd been captured by HEX. I was the one who'd made friends with a mudluff. I'd stumbled into a HEX trap a second time, lost my entire team, been kicked off Inter-World, and somehow regained my memories and found my team again. And I was the first redheaded J-named person to bring someone new to the base. No one else here could say any one of those things, let alone all of them . . . and here I was again, standing out, with my girl friend (not "girlfriend," mind you) and my mudluff friend, wandering through the halls like I hadn't a care in the world.

Really, it was no wonder some of my para-incarnations still disliked me.

"Deep thoughts?" asked Acacia, and I realized I was neglecting my duties as tour guide. We'd passed through several hallways without my saying a word, not that there'd been anything interesting to say about them. They were hallways. Some of them had doors that led to other hallways.

"No, sorry. Just thinking about . . . the mess hall. You're

gonna get swarmed," I warned her, unsurprised when she merely assured me she'd be fine.

"I can handle it," she said—and then I opened the door.

Okay, so I'd like to say a mob of redheaded, freckle-faced Walkers surged forward like paparazzi, asking questions and clamoring for our attention. It's what I was expecting, honestly. In retrospect, I'm pretty sure Acacia *would* have been able to handle that, no problem. What actually happened was like something out of one of those old horror movies, or teen chick flicks where there's the dreaded embarrassing school scene.

I opened the door, and all noise stopped.

Just *stopped*. Everyone stopped talking. One after the other, everyone trailed off in the middle of a sentence, all eyes turning to Acacia and me.

Then, like a wave rolling slowly over the shore, the chatter started up again—muted, hushed—from one end of the room to the other. Slowly, most of them turned back to what they were doing—eating or chatting or reading or enjoying some kind of handheld media—and the noise level rose again, though nowhere near to what it had been before.

It was probably one of the most unnerving things I'd ever experienced, and that's saying a lot.

Acacia seemed to be of much the same opinion. I didn't think anyone could tell from inside the room, but she was leaning slightly toward me. Hue was practically settled on my shoulder like a parrot, but he tended to do that when we were around a bunch of people.

"This is the mess," I said to Acacia, not bothering to raise or lower my voice. I was just giving her a tour; it didn't need to be a big deal. "Kitchen's open. It's not gourmet, but most of the stuff tastes okay when you get used to it."

"Let me guess: vitamin-enriched condensed protein?" Acacia walked casually over to the buffet table with me.

"Yep. Just like Mom used to make," I joked, noting that the mention of Mom only brought a slight pang of homesickness instead of the crippling, gut-wrenching sadness it used to cause. I didn't know how to feel about that, or about Acacia's knowing look.

"Yeah," she agreed, her expression contrasting with something a little softer in her voice. "If Mom was an army chef."

I watched her pile food onto her tray with reckless abandon, apparently not needing any help to figure out what was what. Or she just didn't care. She was hard to read, and I didn't want it to look like I was trying. A sudden instinct for chivalry bubbled up from somewhere inside me, and I carried her water glass and protein shake to a table for her. She hadn't asked, and didn't do anything other than look faintly surprised as I took them, but she gave me a nod of thanks as I set them down. I still wasn't sure where the instinct had come from, but the simple nod—not sarcastic, not teasing, not anything but grateful—made me glad I'd done it.

"I actually love these," she commented as she bit into a grainberry, one of the few Earth-grown things on the menu.

I couldn't stand them, but I kept that to myself. "So, where are you from?" I'd refrained from asking thus far, certain I wouldn't get a real answer, but I was dying of curiosity. How did she know so much about InterWorld and every other world?

"Around," she answered, with a mysterious smile and that little shrug. The smile was kind of enticing, like she was daring me to ask more.

"Well, how old are you?"

"That's *so* rude. Do they not teach you manners on this boat?"

"Several cultures' worth," I informed her, for once thinking fast enough to keep up. "And in some places, direct questions are a sign of respect."

She took a drink from her shake, giving me that faintly appraising up-and-down look. "I'm not from one of them," she said finally, but she still sounded playful.

"Okay. That narrows it down to a few million different possibilities." Despite her continued lack of real answers to any of my questions, I was enjoying the game. I didn't actually mind that she wasn't telling me anything. I just wanted to learn more about her, and even though I wasn't getting any *facts*, I was learning what she was like. It was something.

I wasn't the only interested party, though, and after

keeping a respectful distance for a while, people started trickling over. The crippling social anxiety I suddenly felt was alleviated by the fact that not one person used the word "girlfriend" in front of Acacia, which made me feel both profoundly grateful and incredibly confused. They'd teased me to no end without her there; wouldn't it be more fun to tease me in front of her?

Maybe not, on second thought. Despite the fact that we all came from very different places, we were all basically the same person, and I know *I'd* been humiliated enough times in school that I wouldn't do the same to my worst enemy, let alone to one of my para-incarnations. It was actually kind of comforting, and I found that now that I wasn't wrestling with social paranoia, I was enjoying seeing Acacia give the other versions of me the same kind of runaround I'd been getting.

"How long are you going to be here?" someone finally asked: Jirho, a smallish version of me who came from a darker, colder version of Earth. He had big, pale eyes and a light coating of fur all along his skin, which basically made him look like me if I were a stuffed animal. He also had claws and pointed canines, and hadn't taken well to the nickname "Plushie."

"Until I'm called back."

"To where?"

"Where I came from."

Hue (who had shrunk to the size of a baseball and settled himself in the hood of my jacket for most of this time) suddenly floated up beside my left ear and disappeared with a faint pop. I blinked, automatically turning my head toward the noise—and the familiar sound of the alarm went off, pinging twice to silence us. Then the Old Man's voice came over the PA system.

"Walkers, we have a Code Mercury."

All noise in the room, which had already lowered to a few murmurs, stopped completely. In the entire time I'd been at InterWorld, we'd *never* had a Code Mercury. I knew what it was, of course, as I was versed in all technical terms and alerts and procedures.

They'd found a Walker—undiscovered by Binary or HEX—on one of the fringe worlds.

CHAPTER SIX

JUST SO YOU UNDERSTAND exactly what a huge deal this was, let me explain some things. The Multiverse is *everything*, all the infinite possibilities and worlds that ever have existed, or might, or will exist. The Altiverse is a comparatively small part of that, a swirling maelstrom that contains all the infinite possible *Earths* that have existed, or might, or will exist.

Then, there's the Arc. Think of it like a crescent moon—you can only see part of it, but the rest of the moon is still there, shadowed. The Arc is the bright part: a slice of the whole picture, the visible worlds that exist on the spectrum. The dark part is where all the possibilities and probabilities exist, those little alternate realities that get split off every time a major decision is made.

One side of the Arc is heavy with magic, the other with technology. The Earths existing around either side of the

Arc are known as the fringe worlds. Fringe worlders are all the more valuable because the worlds they come from are so heavily influenced with science or magic that the Walkers tend to be more powerful than us middle worlders. The ones who come from the magic side can do anything from fly to cast spells, and I'm not talking like Jo can fly, with wings if there's enough magic in the air. I mean just *fly*, because they will it to be so. Because they're magic enough to manage it even without the atmosphere they're used to. Ones from the science spectrum are more like J/O—from what I've heard, he's the closest to a fringer we've gotten in a few decades.

The fringe worlds almost never yield Walkers anymore; HEX and Binary hold sway on opposite ends of the spectrum, and they grab up all the Walkers they can find. Sometimes we get a blip here and there, but we've never been able to get out there before they get snatched up.

The giant screen at the back of the mess hall was alight, and every eye was on it. Would the new Walker be from the magic end or the science? How long before Binary or HEX would find them?

"We don't know their status yet, but Upstairs leads me to believe it has the potential to be disastrous if we don't get them. Joeb, Jerzy, Jonha, Jorisine, and Josy—suit up."

A low murmur went through the room. Four of those names were senior field ops, and no one had *ever* heard of the Old Man sending that many at once on *any* mission. If this failed, four teams would be off the grid until they could be split and reassigned.

This was *huge*.

He was sending the heavy hitters, too. Joeb was from one of the fringe worlds himself, on the magic side. Come to think of it, that probably meant this Earth was magic heavy; Joeb looked more or less human, but Jonha had skin like tree bark and Jorisine was the closest thing to an elf I'd ever met. Josy also looked more or less human, except I privately liked to think of her as Rapunzel. Her golden hair went down to her feet, and was stronger than anything I'd ever encountered. She wore it in a bunch of thin braids, with little knives tied into the ends.

As for the last one, birdlike Jerzy was light, quick, and one of the fastest runners on Base. He couldn't fly like Jo, but as fast as he could move, he didn't need to. I was actually kind of proud that he was going on an officer team; Jerzy had been one of the first friends I'd made here, and I hoped this meant he might be considered for officer status later.

"Everyone is expected to sleep with one eye open tonight; while the chance of anyone tracing us is slim, the possibility does exist, especially with the power we're about to expend. Joey Harker, assemble your team and report to my office."

The screen went dark, and it took me a moment to register what I'd just heard.

"Did he say *my* name?" I managed smartly, looking at

Josef. He and Jakon were the only members of my team still up, as far as I was aware.

"Sure did," Josef confirmed, though he looked as confused as I felt.

"We can't be going out again; we were out this morning." Jakon was still staring at the screen, fur ruffled slightly in her confusion.

"Well, we won't find out by sitting here." I sighed, getting to my feet. "Let's go. The others probably heard all that, too. Let's not make them wait."

"Good luck," Acacia offered, and I stared at her for a moment before I remembered to say thanks. I'd forgotten she was there. Which raised a slight problem.

"Right, you're . . . supposed to be escorted at all times, aren't you?"

"Don't worry about it. I'll stay in the mess." She nodded to the people still sitting around; though less than there had been at dinner, there were still quite a few. "I'm not done eating yet."

"Okay," I said, pausing to consider. She wasn't *technically* my responsibility, so I wouldn't get in trouble if I left her . . . and the order to assemble my team had come from the Old Man himself, so I was covered. I nodded, offering a "Well, see ya," as I headed out. Not the most debonair exit I'd ever made, but I was tired and distracted. It didn't seem like this day would *ever* end.

"She's coming," Jakon said after a moment, perking up. We'd only been standing outside the Old Man's office for about thirty seconds, but even five seems like an eternity when you know he's waiting for you.

Jo rounded the corner a second later at a jog, her hair looking somewhat puffier than usual. As she got closer to us, we could see that her wings were damp, the feathers looking far more scraggly than majestic. "Sorry," she muttered as she slowed, raking some of her hair back from her face. "I was in the shower," she said defensively as we all glanced at one another.

"Mm, wet feather smell," Jakon teased her, earning an annoyed glance.

"You're one to talk," she replied, with that aristocratic haughtiness that only beings with wings seem able to muster.

"We're going in now," I said, opening the door.

Jai was already inside, standing silently with his hands behind his back. He didn't even glance up as we came in. His gaze was fixed on the picture hanging behind the Old Man's desk, the one of the Arc that was the Altiverse. The Old Man himself gave us one of his signature glares as we entered.

"Glad you decided to join us. Don't sit, you're suiting up."

"But we were—" Jakon started, then fell immediately silent as he turned to her.

"I am aware of your schedule, Jakon Haarkanen, seeing

as I *make it*." He let the reprimand settle for a moment, waiting to see if she was stupid enough to say anything else. She wasn't.

"You're going back to Earth FΔ98[6]. You're going back for three very specific reasons, not the least of which is *because I say so*. The other two I am telling you so you will grasp the importance of your mission and hopefully not fail again." He let that sink in before continuing. "First, you are to succeed in your initial mission. We *need* that data." He turned his gaze to J/O. As our resident computer whiz, he was to be the one responsible for hacking into the mainframe and downloading the files we needed. *Why* we needed them, we didn't know—and we didn't ask. The Old Man gave information out on a need-to-know basis, which meant that grunts like us were rarely ever in the loop.

"The second is another Code Mercury. A Walker blipped the radar an hour or so ago. The Binary already has him, but it's on the same world you just came from—you probably stirred him up with your rapid entrance and exit. He's a powerful one, too. *Get him*."

We all nodded, but I couldn't help thinking that this didn't make sense. There were *two* Walkers, surfacing at the same time? I wasn't sure that had ever happened, but if the other one was yet undiscovered, why send *four* officers after him and leave *us* to fight our way through the Binary's forces?

The Old Man turned to look at me, and I could feel my

skin prickle as if I were sunburned. "You have something to say, Harker?"

No attainment in feigning disingenuousness, as Jai would say. "Yes, sir. Sir—if the Binary already has him at one of their bases, why are you sending *us* and not the four officers you sent after—"

His intensity racheted up a notch, and my skin went from bad sunburn to slow roast. "Because, despite the twofold importance of this mission, the other Walker is the priority. Believe me when I say it was a difficult decision.

"I know you've been out already, but have a latte and get back to it. Jai has all the information, and the alchemist will meet you in the locker room. Dismissed."

We filed out of his office, stepping onto the conveyer. Walking was encouraged except in emergencies; most of the halls had strips of moving floor that could be adjusted to various speeds. I pathed it to the lockers and upped it a few notches; we'd get there in a matter of seconds rather than the two or three minutes it would have taken us to walk.

Sometimes those minutes make the difference.

Jirathe was waiting with our lattes—the informal term for booster shots—and didn't bother wasting words as we suited up. She gave us each a jolt, watching our reactions carefully. I don't know what's in them; she told me once, but the chemical names meant nothing to me. All I know is that they provided an extra juice that left you feeling like you'd had ten hours' sleep on a mattress so wonderful even Hans Christian Andersen's snotty princess couldn't kvetch about it, but without the crash and burn that you usually wound up with.

We stepped onto the platform at the edge of the lockers. The huge automatic doors slid open, revealing the prehistoric Earth beneath us, the last rays of dying light filtering in, along with a breath of fresh air. Jirathe burst into a thousand colors behind us, and we Walked.

"Did your world have movies? Because there's this movie from my world called *Mission: Impossible*, and it has this really catchy theme music—"

Jai gritted his teeth, knuckles turning white as he clasped his hands in front of him. "Kindly cease your superfluous prattle," he muttered to me, not taking his eyes off Jakon. "This requires an inordinate amount of concentration."

"Sorry," I responded. There wasn't much else I could say. Jakon was scaling the outside of the building while Jai made her invisible. Or, as he'd explained it, "Depreciated the probability of her being discovered." He wasn't making her invisible so much as he was surrounding her with the belief that she couldn't be seen. It was hard to believe, considering *we* could all see her as she made her way up the wall, but Jai had explained that we were able to see her because we knew she was there already. What I didn't know was *how* she was climbing it; the building was glass and metal, and straight as a ruler. She was apparently accomplishing it on nothing more than clean thoughts and pure intentions.

J/O spoke up, confirming that Jakon had successfully planted the microchip that would scramble the security system. He put a hand to the panel next to the door, eyes unfocusing for a moment as he sorted through the command system.

After our last attempt, we'd decided to try a different approach. We knew they had the advantage of numbers— well, they always had that, but this time by hundreds instead of dozens—but we had something we hadn't bothered to use before. All their attention would be diverted to keeping the new Walker contained, and no one would expect us to come back soon after our harrowing escape just this morning. The Binary were all organic computers; they calculated what was logical, and likely. They were the closest thing to the Borg we'd found—well, except for Universe YYΣ237^3, which most of us just called the Trekiverse. At any rate, we were humans (most of us), and we had emotion. We also had determination. Last but not least, we had the element of surprise.

We also had a shot each of latte, which was probably how Jakon was able to literally climb the wall.

"Let's go," Jo said, bouncing a little on her toes. She was acting more like Jakon than her usual calm, slightly sarcastic self.

"Not yet," I cautioned, though I was just as eager to get this over with as the rest of them. "Wait until J/O—"

"Got it," the cyborg said, his eyes refocusing as the doors slid shut. "Jakon's upstairs in a vent, but her portable scrambler will keep her hidden from the patrol bots. The Walker's on the same floor as the information we need."

"How fortuitous," Jai said. I couldn't help but agree with him, and that worried me. I wasn't sure if I was just being paranoid or not, but the last time I'd been worried on a mission, my entire team had been captured by an elaborate HEX-laid trap. "Just keep an eye out," I cautioned, earning a semidisgusted look from J/O.

"Do you doubt my sensors?"

"No, I just don't want all of us to end up in a HEX sandwich again."

"We're dealing with the Binary this time, not HEX."

"It would probably taste the same: bad."

Jo giggled, and Josef laughed. Even Jai smirked a little. We were all a bit loopy. Our senses were working well enough, though. Twice on our way up the stairs we used Jai's "we're not really here" trick to avoid a clone patrol, and once J/O projected an image of an empty hallway to fool a patrol bot. In some ways, the Binary was easier to deal with than HEX; computers made more sense to me than magic, even though I wasn't full of nanochips like J/O was.

There were downsides, however.

"Crap."

"You've got *how* many dictionaries in your head, and that's all you can come up with? . . . What's wrong?"

J/O simply pointed. At a wall.

We stared for a moment at the wall, then at one another. Then at J/O.

"Did you blow a fuse or something?" Jo finally asked. "What are we looking at?"

"What does it look like? It's a wall," J/O said quite helpfully, and I think someone would have tried to strangle him, if he'd needed to breathe. Luckily for him, he continued before any of us could come up with a more effective way of venting our frustration. "It's supposed to be a door, guys."

"Not all of us have the floor plans in an embedded mission file," I snapped.

"Not my fault." J/O looked smug.

"Just project it, already."

One of his eyes glowed red for a moment, then a map of the building appeared on the wall closest to us. There was a little gray dot in the corridor that served as J/O's "you are here" beacon, and in front of it was a door. Except the door existed only on the map, not in reality.

"Hm," said Jai. He took a step forward, but didn't get any further than that before the wall opened, with no fanfare, to reveal Jakon.

The wolf girl was crouched on top of a clone guard, her

arm still outstretched from where she'd pushed the button to activate the concealed door. Several more guards were stretched out across the floor behind her, the satisfied smirk on her face making their fate obvious.

"What took you so long?" she asked.

"Good job, girl! You want a treat?" Josef was the only one of us who dared to tease her like that, since he'd demonstrated exactly once that he was big enough (and strong enough) to pick her up by the scruff of the neck. She bared her teeth and growled at him, though it lacked her usual oomph. She was amused. So was I, but I couldn't help wondering what the point of the one-way door had been. Why have a room you could get out of but not into?

"Is this the computer you need, J/O?" I asked as we filed into the room. "And can you project that map again? I want to make sure there aren't any other hidden doors in here."

"An adroit cogitation, Joey," Jai said as the map appeared on the wall again.

"*Joe*, remember?" I studied the map. I wasn't the best at reading them, but this seemed fairly straightforward. J/O's little gray dot was in the middle of the room; behind it was the door we'd come in; and there were three walls, all smooth and doorless. Everything looked normal—except for several dotted lines going through the picture. "What are those?"

"Vent shafts. How else do you think Jakon got in?"

"Follow this one," I said, tapping my finger along one of

the dotted lines. Then I forgot about the mystery of the door-less room as a new thought occurred to me. "Do you know *exactly* where the new Walker is?"

J/O's other eye narrowed in concentration; then another gray blip appeared on the map, a few rooms and hallways over from where we were. "The shafts go right to it. We could send Jakon back up there."

"Sure," the wolf girl said, flashing a toothy grin.

"Your plan is sound, but J/O needs to devote his attention to the computers at this juncture. I would suggest we separate to accomplish both objectives."

Jai was right. I didn't want to split up the party, but we had a time limit here. The miniscrambler Jakon had placed and the one she was carrying meant they hadn't discovered us yet, but J/O had been able to make only two, and they weren't very powerful. His hacking into the system would likely ring the first alarm, and us rescuing the Walker would trigger the second.

"We've gotta do this at the same time," I decided. "Jo, can you fit in the shaft with your wings?"

Jo looked at Jakon, who narrowed her eyes thoughtfully, then nodded. "They fold," Jo said somewhat reluctantly.

"Good. Jo, Jakon, and I will go through the vents to get the Walker. Josef and Jai will guard J/O while he downloads the data. Jai, let's you and me link."

Jai nodded, putting one hand out, the other to his ear.

I did the same, and we touched palms. An odd metallic "taste" touched my mind. It was kind of like when you go swimming for too long and the chlorine starts to feel like it's part of you.

Testing, I thought at Jai, who nodded.

Your projected voice is perfectly discernible.

"I wish linking gave me access to even half your vocabulary," I said out loud. Then I turned to Jakon and Jo. "Ready, girls?" At their nods, I glanced over to Josef. "Can you give us a boost?"

The big man nodded, lifting Jakon with one hand. She scrambled up into the vent shaft, hardly making a sound. I went next, unfortunately with a little more noise—Jakon was lighter than I was and a sight more graceful. I silently resolved to be more careful with my weight distribution; the last thing we needed was to have the vent creak and give us away. Jakon looked smug as I slipped carefully past her to take the lead, testing my weight against the metal sheeting.

Jo came up next, her wings folded around her like a cloak. The shaft was too small for me to turn and look at her, but I got the sense that she was irritated. I remembered how she said she'd just gotten out of the shower, and made sure to keep my mirth to myself. She'd need another one after this. "Jakon, do you have your blaster?"

"Yeah," she growled, in the universal tone for "duh."

"Good. Pass it to me. When Jai gives the signal, I'll activate my shield and go in first. The shield'll take the first few hits; I should be able to take out some of them in that time. After you hear the first four or five shots, you come down and do your thing. The room we're headed to has an outside window—it's on the left. As soon as either of us is able, we break it. Jo, when you hear the glass shatter, you come down and get the Walker. Just fly him out—"

"I can't fly here," she said. "I can glide, but—"

"Then do that! Find the nearest portal and get back to Base. Got it?"

Jakon nodded. Jo hesitated for a moment, obviously unsure about the idea of leaving us there, but gave a quiet "okay."

We continued on through the vents in silence—and then came to something I hadn't anticipated.

The vent split, going left and right.

"Which way?" Jakon whispered, and I took a deep breath, trying to picture J/O's map on the wall. If we'd been facing that way, and the vents went up . . . But I'd been moving my finger sideways along the wall, which wasn't the same thing as "up," and it seemed like we were going another way now. Was it left?

I wasn't sure.

"Joey! Which way?" Jakon's voice was now a hiss, and I closed my eyes. I'd never been good at this sort of thing.

Why could I walk between worlds and come up with elaborate plans that actually worked sometimes but couldn't read a map?

Wait a minute—it was because I was also an idiot. I didn't need maps. I was a Walker, and so was the person we were going to save.

I took a deep breath, casting about in my mind until I found the thing that enabled me to Walk, and expanded it.

And I felt him. It felt like when we were on the *Malefic* and we'd freed the spirits of our brothers and sisters, set them loose from the jars. . . . My brain felt like it was full of static, and there was a definite magnetic pull, linking me to the captive Walker. Our senses touched, and I knew him. His name was Joaquim.

"Right," I whispered, and Jakon turned. I followed blindly, still buzzing from the adrenaline and the exhilaration of what I'd just done, and the memory of freeing those trapped spirits in our desperate flight from HEX, the first mission that made us a team.

I stopped. We were directly above them. I could feel it.

"Here." I took out Jakon's blaster and mine and braced myself against the side of the shaft with my knees pulled up to my chest.

Jai? Status?

J/O is attempting to bypass the firewall.

Let him trip the alarm, I thought. *As long as he gets the information we need, the alarm will actually help us out.*

There was a pause, then, *Allow us to confer.* Another pause. *As you say. He is disabling the firewall. . . .*

"Ready?" The girls nodded, and I took a breath, waited for Jai's voice in my head—*"Now!"*—and kicked the side of the vent open, activating my shield as I tumbled out in a controlled fall, guns held to either side like an action hero. There were advantages to all of the classes I took at InterWorld, but some of them were better than others.

There were eight to ten guards in the room, all rutabagas—three of them at the only door, a few standing around, and four clustered around the new Walker. I didn't bother aiming for those; too much of a chance I'd hit him. An alarm went off, and I managed to take out one as I landed, and another before they started firing. I felt the blasts ping off my shield, automatically counting—*One—two—*

Out of the corner of my eye I saw the Walker get to his feet, swinging the chair he'd been sitting on like a weapon. It cracked into one of the clones, and I abruptly changed my strategy as two of the others went for him. I was a little surprised, honestly. I'd assumed he'd be terrified by all this. I was, when it had happened to me. Instead, he was drawing some of their fire—and he didn't have a shield.

I zapped the one closest to him, counting off another two shots as they hit my chest and arm. I felt the shield weaken, and perfectly on cue, Jakon tumbled out of the vent with a sound somewhere between a howl and a bark. She landed on one of the clones, hopped off like he was a trampoline, and sank her teeth into a second one. I zapped another of the rutabagas closest to Joaquim, then figured if he was going to be proactive he may as well also be useful.

"The window!" I shouted, and he stared at me. No matter how many times it happened, it was always a shock seeing your own face looking back at you. I wondered, on some level, if twins ever felt that way. Joaquim was less like me than some; his hair and eyes were darker, though still noticeably red and brown, respectively. I saw the same shock and suspicion in his eyes we all feel when this happens, just for a moment—and then he did as I'd suggested, swinging the chair around in an arc to shatter the window.

The glass tumbled outward, along with the chair, and Jo shot out of the vent. Her wings snapped out to either side (along with a cloud of dust that would have been funny in any other situation), and she half flew, half fell over to Joaquim. His eyes went wide as she wrapped her arms around him, taking them both through the window and outside. They disappeared from sight for a moment as they fell, then Jo caught an updraft and soared back into view, the new Walker dangling from her arms. She pumped her wings once, twice, gained altitude—and a blaster went off behind me, the shot going wild as Jakon pounced on one of the clones. It zipped past me, taking what was left of my shield, and searing through Jo's right wing.

She dropped, leaving only a few dusty feathers suspended in the sky.

CHAPTER SEVEN

I REMEMBER BEING IN a car accident once. Mom was driving, and the person in front of us slammed on his brakes to avoid a ball that had rolled out into the middle of the street. I hadn't been paying attention, but I remember hearing Mom say *"No—!"* as our car skidded on the pavement, in this tone that was somewhere between the firm, no-nonsense Mommy voice and the pleading, "no-it's-not-time-for-bed" voice my little sister would use. I remember how I knew something was very wrong a second before our car hit the other one. We hadn't been going too fast, so the accident wasn't bad—more than the crash itself, I've never forgotten hearing Mom say *no* that way, as though she could stop the car by will alone. She hadn't remembered that she'd said it, afterward.

It's human instinct to react to a bad situation, regardless of how effective that reaction is. Some people move, some freeze, some hold their breath or gasp or yell. Our combat teacher was always saying that everyone had instinct, it was just a matter of training it, honing it to do what would most benefit you and your teammates in any situation.

So when Jo disappeared from the sky, I didn't waste time with words. Knowing Jakon would take care of the clone behind me, I reached down to the shield disk at my belt, activating the charger. A fully charged shield could take several plasma blasts, a few spells, and maybe twenty pounds of blunt force. They took ten seconds to fully charge. I had about as long as it would take me to get to the window.

I sprinted over, catching myself on the frame with one hand, watching as they fell through the air. Jo had spread both wings out, trying to slow their fall, her arms still wrapped around the new Walker. *"Jo!"* I yelled. It had been two seconds. Three. Four . . .

She folded one wing, turning as she fell so she could see me. I pulled the shield free of the charger and hurled it, Frisbee style, toward her. I saw her grit her teeth as she pumped her wings again, trying to delay the inevitable long enough for it to reach her. We both knew it wasn't fully charged; at best, she and the Walker would come out of it with several broken bones. *If* it got to her before they hit the ground.

Joaquim had his arms wrapped around her waist. She managed to free a hand, and reached out toward the disk. I was glad my father had taught me how to throw; my aim was good, but she had too much of a head start. It wasn't going to reach her in time—

A look of shock crossed her face. Her body seemed to ripple, just for an instant, as did the air around her—and then they vanished, the disk passing through the air where they'd been. It hit the ground a second later.

"She Walked," Jakon said from beside me. "She's okay. She Walked."

I closed my eyes and cast about for the familiar tug of a portal, heart still pounding from the adrenaline.

"Are you sure? I don't sense a portal anywhere—"

"When were you looking for one?"

"Just now—"

"Then she used it, and you wouldn't sense it now, because it's gone. Just like we need to be. Come on!" She tugged at my shirt, pulling me back to the center of the room, though not before I caught a glimpse of clones filing out of the doors downstairs, trying to find the girl they'd just seen falling from the sky. Everyone in the building knew we were here—it was definitely time to go.

Jakon boosted me up into the vent, then leaped up herself. We scrambled back the way we came, not bothering to be quiet. I hoped J/O was done with his download.

Jai, we're coming back.

I got no response, just a jumbled sense of worry and confusion.

Jai!

Hurry, Joey! His voice came back to me, strained. *There's a path here, but it's faint. We need you three and the new one. J/O can't Walk now.*

We're only two—Jo and the Walker are back at Base, I think—

Jai swore, not in a language I knew, but the meaning attached to it in his mind would have made me blush in any other circumstance. *Just get here—*

I tumbled out of the opening Jakon had first used to get into the room, interrupting Jai's mental sentence as I practically landed on top of him. Jakon came down a second later, giving a low, throaty growl. I handed her back her blaster, taking a moment to stare in shock.

Jai and Josef were standing in the center of the room, J/O draped over Josef's shoulder like a sack of bionic potatoes. Jai had his arms out to either side like Gandalf doing his "you-shall-not-pass" speech, and the entire room had come alive.

It was like being inside of a computer, if that computer was also one of those carnival houses where everything popped out at you unexpectedly. The normal things you were used to seeing in a room—light switches, electrical sockets, track lighting, ceiling fans—were all trying to kill us.

I pointed and fired, zapping through a tentacle-like wire that was extending from a wall socket, pulsing blue with electricity. "What happened to J/O?"

"He seemed to experience some kind of—"

"In English, Jai!"

"—He short-circuited! Focus on the path—we have to open a portal!"

I sidestepped to avoid a fan blade as it spun toward me like a psychotic boomerang, simultaneously shooting at one of the lights. This explained the one-way door—the Binary were all electronic entities, and there was a heavy-duty computer tucked up against the wall. Who needed doors when you could plug your consciousness into any electric station in the building? It could let the clones or lesser machines in, but nothing got through that door without it knowing . . . unless they happened to have a mini-scrambler and access to the air vents, like Jakon did.

Okay, one mystery solved. Now for the other—how to get out of here. I planted my feet, once again feeling that little tingle in my mind as I cast about for a portal. There wasn't one here, but energy was strong; sort of like ley lines. In some universe close to this one, a portal existed. The path was there, we just had to walk it. Or, more specifically, Walk it.

"Josef, concentrate!" He was the only other one not entirely devoted to fighting, since he was holding the unconscious J/O. The bigger version of me steadied his blaster, holding it out in front of him and letting training take over as he focused his mind. I felt his power add to mine, the possibility of a portal becoming more of a probability.

"Jakon!"

She backed up against me with a growl, holstering her blaster and using her claws to block the wires and circuits coming for her. She preferred her claws over the blaster, anyway. Her awareness joined ours, the path becoming clear before us.

Now the hard part.

"Jai!"

The more spiritual version of me pulled his arms inward, then thrust them out again. Instead of dropping the shield he'd been sustaining, like I'd expected, he expanded it to include all of us, and joined his mind with ours.

Together, we found that little *something* that was our ticket home, the equation

$$\{IW\}:=\Omega/\infty$$

that told us where to go and how to get there.

And we Walked.

Well, some of us Walked. Some of us were carried, and some of us—like Jai and myself—remember nothing more than the chaotic garishness of the In-Between for a moment before we lost consciousness.

It wasn't the first, second, or even third time I'd woken up in the infirmary. I knew where I was before I opened my eyes, before I really even knew I was awake. It smelled like medicine and cleaning agents, and I could sense others around me. I was fairly certain I knew who they were, and a glance around when I opened my eyes confirmed it—my teammates.

Jai was in the med-bed across from me, still either asleep or unconscious. J/O was on my left side, plugged in to both an IV and a computer, also still unconscious. To my right (and to my great relief) was Jo.

"Hey," I said quietly, and my voice sounded relieved even to me. She glanced up and gave half a smile, which was all I usually got from her. I liked Jo; I had since that day on the cliff, when we'd come to something resembling an understanding about Jay's death. I knew she was indifferent to me at best, but I was glad to have her on my team. "I'm sorry about your wing. How is it?"

She looked up at the damaged appendage, making a face. She was sitting on top of the bed rather than under the covers, leaning back against the pillows, and I could see bandages wrapped around her radius and ulna. Several of her secondary feathers were missing or singed. "Won't be able to fly again for a few days . . . Probably won't be able to fly straight for a few weeks, until they grow back."

"I'm sorry," I said again, not sure what else to say. She glanced back over at me.

"Thanks for trying to throw me the shield. It might've worked."

"Yeah. No problem. You didn't need it, though—smart of you to Walk like that. Good job."

She shook her head. "I didn't. It was the new kid."

I just stared for a moment, letting my brain process this. The new kid had Walked? With Jo? When none of us had sensed a portal? "How?"

"Instinct, I guess. . . . How did we all Walk, the first time?"

I inclined my head slightly, agreeing. I couldn't really say for sure how it had happened—it had just *happened*, which I guess was her point. Thinking about the first time I Walked made me remember something else, and I may have smirked a little. "How'd he take to the In-Between?"

"Dunno . . . I passed out." She looked a little uncomfortable at the admission, and I decided not to press it, but it actually just made me even more curious. The new kid had found his way through the In-Between, by himself, with a wounded Walker?

Okay, I'll admit it. I was impressed.

"How're J/O and Jai?"

"Jai just used too much energy with the shield and trying to Walk. I guess since you two were still linked . . ."

". . . I passed out, too," I finished, and she nodded. I made a face; that had been stupid of us—keeping the link up when we were right there and about to attempt something difficult—but to be fair, we hadn't really had time to take it down. Still, I was going to have to include it in my report anyway, and I was sure the Old Man'd give me one of those *looks* when he read it.

Jo noticed my expression and nodded again—*you deserved that*—but kept talking. "J/O is . . . They think he just ran into some kind of security virus, and it triggered a hard shutdown. They're monitoring him now, but the doctors don't seem too worried."

I nodded. So, all in all, we'd come out okay. Some injuries, some bruises, but we'd gotten the new Walker. And—

"Did he get the data?"

Jo nodded again. "Yeah. Captain Harker is looking it over." Jo was the only one on my team who occasionally called him that instead of the Old Man. It always bothered me to hear, though. My dad had called me that sometimes when I was little. I'd gone through a *Star Trek* phase, and used to pretend I was captain of my own spaceship—the spaceship being the downstairs couch, my bed, the car, or anything else I could think of. I always heard my dad's voice whenever someone said "Captain Harker," and it always weirded me out. Still, it wasn't Jo's fault. She had no way of knowing, though I wondered if her dad had been similar to mine. Parallel worlds were funny that way.

"You file your report yet?" I asked instead, leaning back against the pillow. It wasn't exactly comfortable, as beds went, but it sure beat being stuffed into an air vent.

"Yeah. Wasn't much to do otherwise."

"How long was I out?"

"Only about half an hour, but they put you under again

to monitor your vitals and ease off your link with Jai. It's been about two hours since we got back."

"Okay." I turned my head toward Jai slowly, so as not to aggravate the headache I felt threatening. Now that she mentioned it, I vaguely remembered waking up the first time, being brought through the halls into the infirmary. It was disjointed and hazy, since I'd still been linked with Jai—a little like being two places at once. "How is he?"

"Medics say he overextended himself, but he should be fine once he gets some rest."

I nodded, taking a deep breath before easing my legs over the edge of the bed and pushing myself carefully up. I felt okay, if a little unsteady, but I knew I'd better get to that report as soon as possible. The sooner I turned that in, the sooner I could turn in, too.

"Go on," Jo said, apparently reading my mind, "before he comes in here and tells you to report in person."

"Good idea." The last thing I needed was to have to try and remember all the details of our mission in the face of his unwavering disapproval.

I started for the door, then paused. Her voice had been a lot quieter than usual; kind of listless, and she'd seemed pale and exhausted. "You need anything?" I asked her. She looked surprised, then shook her head. "Just . . . more sleep. I'm fine."

I stepped out and headed to my quarters, inwardly

marveling at how she always seemed shocked when I was nice to her. Granted, we'd never really gotten along, but we hadn't exactly *not*, either. At least, not since I'd told her to stop being a jerk to me. Maybe that had something to do with it.

The halls were empty as I made my way to my room. What time was it, anyway? I glanced at my watch; three A.M. No wonder everything was quiet.

Standing inside my quarters, I noticed something was odd, though it took me a moment to put my finger on it. There was nothing really *wrong*, just . . .

The room was empty. No Hue and no Acacia.

I hadn't even realized I'd been expecting to find her there until I hadn't. Truthfully, I'd mostly forgotten about her since I'd had to focus on the mission . . . but now, alone in my dark, silent room, I was surprised at how disappointed I was. Where was she? Had she gotten her own room? Had she left Base Town?

That last thought almost sent me back out the door, but I stopped myself before I'd even started to turn around. "Don't be ridiculous, Joey," I muttered out loud—and slapped my hand against my forehead in frustration upon realizing that I'd called *myself* "Joey." No wonder it was proving impossible to get other people to think of me as "Joe"; I couldn't even remember to think of myself that way.

"Write your report and go to bed," I told myself, half expecting someone to answer me. My room remained silent, so I went over to my desk and settled down in front of my computer, which was really more of a glorified typewriter. Forget computer games or the internet—this thing was fast as a nanopod, but it didn't do anything other than type and print.

"Mission 2 to Earth F delta ninety-eight to the sixth," I muttered at I typed. "Joe Harker." I looked at my name for a moment, then added a *y*. Then I deleted it. Then I erased the whole thing and wrote *Joseph*. Nice and neutral. After all, the Old Man had introduced himself to me as Joe Harker, and there was no sense in getting confusing.

I stared at the blank screen for a moment, then started to type.

The only thing more infuriating than playing second fiddle to the new kid on campus was when you'd *rescued* the new kid and gotten no credit for it. Not only was Joaquim the new Hero of Base Town, he was arguably the coolest version of me I'd ever met, and he knew it. He was taking to the whole thing with an unruffled calm that was confounding at the best of times, and made me want to toss him into the Hazard Zone with high percentage variables and no weapon every time he retold the tale of how he'd saved Jo.

Of course, he was only retelling the story because his fellow Walkers *asked* him to. He would never think of bragging or talking himself up. He let everyone else do that for him.

Now, it's not like I was ever the big man on campus. I had been shunned for a lot of my first few months, and even after I *had* single-handedly rescued my team from the clutches of HEX and helped them destroy a siege ship that would have made Darth Vader cry for his mommy, I'd gotten nothing more than the satisfaction of having people occasionally sit next to me in the mess or nod when I passed them in the hall. Surely no one had asked me to tell *my* story over and over again.

What made it worse was that while he was being congratulated for saving Jo and making it back on his own, *I* was being crucified for losing the shield disk.

I'd finished my report early that morning and left my room to drop it by the Old Man's office, after I'd made sure I didn't have any key-shaped imprints on my face. Falling asleep at your keyboard ("waffle-facing," we called it) was considered a newbie incident, and the last thing I wanted was someone teasing me about it this morning. I'd had enough of teasing the day before.

I hadn't even made it to the mess hall before Jernan, the quartermaster, found me. He proceeded to give me a ten-minute dressing-down about the importance of equipment and keeping it clean, working, and most of all, *here*. Trying to explain that it had been to save Jo—and the new Walker—was in vain.

After becoming the new poster boy for what *not* to do on a mission, I sat down with my breakfast. There was no wrong way to eat breakfast, and Altiverse help anyone who tried to tell me otherwise.

"Ew, grits. Who eats *that*?"

I shouldn't have been surprised. No matter where I went, Acacia "not Casey" Jones was there to throw a wrench into my well-oiled nerves.

I turned with a ready retort, only to have it die as she sat down next to me with her own bowl of grits. She winked, and I couldn't help a slight smile in return, my attention going immediately back to my breakfast. I was suddenly a lot less glad to see her this morning than I would've been last night.

"Hey, what's wrong?"

"Nothing. It's been a *day*."

"It's not even nine yet."

"Well, my day didn't end until about four A.M. yesterday, and I got up at six. So it's still a day, as far as I'm concerned."

"You're grumpy when you don't sleep," she teased, and I couldn't help feeling a little under fire.

"What do you want me to say?" I guess my voice was more snappish than I meant it to be, because the way she spat out her reply might as well have been a slap to the face.

"I don't care what you say, but stop saying it like I'm the bad guy."

I took a breath, and a drink of vitamin water. "Sorry."

"What's got you all inverted?"

"I just had a really long day yesterday, that's all. And

Jernan—the QM—is furious with me for losing a shield disk."
At her questioning glance, I sighed and explained. "I tried to
throw it to Jo when she fell—"

"Which was a good move, by the way." Most of the time
it was impossible to tell who was speaking unless you looked
at them. I mean, we all had pretty much the exact same
voice, give or take some quirks. This one sounded *exactly* like
me, yet I still wasn't at all surprised when Joaquim sat down
across from us. I knew it'd be him, probably because that was
how my luck was going lately.

"I mean, I had no idea what it *was* when you threw it
at us," he continued, spearing a bit of something made to
look like eggs on his fork. "But I made the connection when
people were talking about you losing the shield disk."

My dismay probably showed on my face, because he
winced and looked sympathetic. "Sorry. But they are talking
about it."

"Of course they are. All anyone ever talks about is what
I do wrong, if they talk about me at all." Acacia raised an
eyebrow at me, but I ignored her.

"Hey, come on," Joaquim said. "I'm the new kid now—I'm
sure I'll be messing up all over the place."

I snorted. "You're already the hero, saving Jo like that." It
rankled me to admit it to his face, but I had to. It was true,
and it was the kind of thing we all needed to hear. "That was
impressive."

"Thank you. I was terrified," he admitted, and I felt some of my jealousy give a bit. "I had no idea what was going on, and it was all so unreal . . . then I got to that crazy place, like . . . It was like . . ."

"An M. C. Escher painting on acid?" I cut in.

"Exactly." He laughed. "Boy, I'm glad you said that. Everyone's been talking about things I don't understand."

"I'm glad you got it," I admitted. "We're all from different worlds, some more different than others. It's hard to find a common pop culture reference sometimes."

"Yeah, I asked someone if we were a team of X-Men, and she looked at me in utter disgust. I don't think she got it."

I laughed. "Where are you from, then?"

"Earth, uh . . . ." He lifted his arm and pulled back his sleeve; I caught a glimpse of hastily scrawled writing on his skin. "$F\Delta98^6$, the captain said."

"Just call him the Old Man. Everyone does. And that's not going to help you with taking tests here," I informed him, indicating the notes on his arm.

"Never did," he replied, looking a little sheepish. "I have the feeling I'm going to fall *way* behind."

"It's not so bad." Damn it—I was liking him more and more, despite my initial decision not to. "Mostly a lot of memorizing, but we're good at that. I mean, I am, so that means you are, right?"

"I guess so. Man, I can't . . . I mean, you're me. You look

like me. *Everyone* here is me."

"I'm not," Acacia spoke up, and I had to admit I'd almost forgotten she was there.

"I was going to ask about that. Are you . . ." He paused, and she just looked at him with a faintly amused, expectant look. "Who are you?"

"Acacia Jones," she offered.

"Don't call her 'Casey,'" I advised, and he grinned. She elbowed me in the side, a little harder than necessary.

"Acacia Jones, the mystery of InterWorld," said a new voice, and I glanced up to see Jerzy. The birdlike version of me was holding a single plate instead of a tray, with a modest amount of food on it.

"I'm just a mystery in general," she told him, winking. His feathers ruffled a bit—mine would have, too, if I'd had any. Probably for a different reason, though.

"Or so you like to make us think." He smirked at her; Jerzy wasn't one to take crap from anyone, pretty girls included. "You work hard on your image, huh?"

"Don't have to," she replied cheerfully. "You guys are all doing it for me."

Joaquim snorted. I decided I liked him a little bit more. Jerzy joined us at the table.

"How'd the retrieval go?" I asked him. The officer team had arrived with the other Walker midmorning, and everyone was dying to get a glimpse of him or her. No such luck—the new one had been taken to the infirmary for a checkup, and then straight to the Old Man's office. No one had heard from him or her since.

"It was awesome!" Jerzy said, glancing briefly at Acacia. His bright red hair feathers were ruffed up, like a peacock trying to attract a mate. "Pretty crazy, actually."

"Yeah?" I prompted.

"Yeah. Josy lost a braid."

"Oooh." I winced. Josy was *vain* about her hair. "How dead's the thing that did it?"

"All the way dead." Jerzy laughed. "It was some kind of plant thing. We were in really lush jungle area with lots of weird, carnivorous vines. Got the Walkers out okay; was mostly a lot of hiding. HEX had a fix on them like nothin' else."

Something was nagging at me. After a moment, I had it. "Walkers?"

Jerzy's feathers ruffled in excitement. "Yeah. It's not released officially yet, so if I hear it spread I'll know where it came from." He paused to look at Acacia (who mimed zipping her mouth closed) and Joaquim, who nodded. "But the new Walker are Walk*ers*. Two of them. Fraternal twins."

My jaw dropped. "Has that ever happened before?"

"Don't think so! And then the Old Man sending you off after a third Walker . . ." He nodded to Joaquim. "Three at once is totally unheard of. Not impossible, of course. But to get two fringers *and* a third at one time . . . Joeb said it was a good day." Jerzy raised his glass to Joaquim in a toast.

"Wow," I managed, still stymied. "And, hey, look at you, off with an officer team!" I clinked my own glass against his, after Joaquim did. "You gonna get promoted?"

He turned a little red. "Not for a while, if it even happens. But it was *awesome* getting to see them in action," he admitted. "Joeb's a great leader. The new ones trusted him immediately. I would've, too."

"That's how it was when I saw Joey," Joaquim agreed, and I was glad enough for the praise that I didn't bother asking him to call me Joe. "I mean, after I realized I wasn't looking at a mirror." He smiled at me. I returned it, remembering my earlier thought about whether or not twins ever had that same problem. Well, now I'd be able to ask some!

"Twins from a fringe world, huh?" I said, still marveling at the odds. "What are they like?"

"Right now, pretty confused! They're handling it all right, though. They've got each other, that's grounding them in some reality. Names're Jari and Jarl, girl and boy. Old Man's gonna release an announcement about them."

As if on cue, the loudspeaker pinged above us.

"Nice," I told Jerzy, as though he'd planned it. He preened a little, and Acacia giggled. The second the Old Man came on the loudspeaker, though, our mirth faded. His voice was serious, the kind of tone that wasn't at all loud but made everyone stop and *listen*.

"Walkers, sit tight. One of our security systems has picked up an anomaly on the graph, and we're taking no chances of being discovered. We're punching it. I know most of you are in the middle of breakfast, so hold on to your plates. Punching in five."

The speaker crackled, then pinged off. A low murmur went through the crowd, some of the voices amused or complaining, a select few who hadn't been through a punch expressing confusion—Acacia included.

"What does he mean, 'we're punching it'?"

"You'll see," I told her, pleased I finally knew something she didn't. "You don't get airsick, do you?"

She fixed me with a withering look, but held on to both her tray and drink, as Jerzy and I were doing. Joaquim did the same, looking confused.

A second later, reality exploded.

That was the best way to describe it, really. "Punching it" basically meant throwing the engines and the interdimensional relocator into overdrive simultaneously. We were traveling through worlds, realities, and possibilities at a few light-years per hour, while sitting still. It would be kind of like taking all the remakes you could find of the same movie, overlaying them on the same projector, and playing them all on fast-forward. The ship around us flickered in and out—it was day and night thirty times in a single second; a flock of birds appeared in the middle of the room and were gone almost too quickly to see; trees appeared and vanished. We were all underwater and none of us were wet. It was like being on the fastest, craziest 3-D roller coaster ever invented. I glanced over to Acacia to see if she was enjoying the ride.

She wasn't. Her eyes were wide and she had her hands to her head, as though trying to block out the world's worst headache. Her odd, circuit-board nails were pulsing with little charges, and she seemed to be flickering out of time with the rest of us. I could see her through the scenery, then I could see the ship through her, which wasn't right.

She was out of sync.

"Hey," I yelled, trying to be heard over the dull roar of the wind, the engines, and the beeping of the alarm.

She turned toward me, dark hair whipping around her face. She started to reach out, then pulled back at the same time I did. We both knew it was a bad idea. If she was off sync, we weren't phasing together—and if we phased into the same space at the same time, things could get pretty messy. "What's wrong?" I yelled.

Her mouth moved, but I couldn't hear her. She frowned, took in a sharp breath, eyes squeezing shut. The ship lurched, I lost my grip on my tray, and the lights dimmed into blackness for a moment as the engines powered down.

The lights came back a second later, bringing with them the usual reaction from the room full of Walkers. Relief or disappointment that it was over, some laughter at those who had lost their breakfast (figuratively or literally; some of us had stronger stomachs than others). Everything was back to normal.

And Acacia was gone.

CHAPTER EIGHT

"SORRY," I APOLOGIZED AS Joaquim wiped the grits off his shirt. I'd let go of my tray during the warp, which was another newbie mistake. It had slid right across the table, only to be stopped by Joaquim. Now he looked like someone had tried to make an abstract painting out of breakfast on him.

"No problem," he said easily. "I'm just glad I didn't throw up. That was nuts."

"Always is," I said, looking around. "Did you see where Acacia went?" It was kind of absurd, but I was fervently hoping she'd somehow just slipped off to the bathroom when the lights were out, or something.

Jerzy and Joaquim shook their heads, and Jerzy gave me a surprisingly serious look, for him. "No, but you should go report it. She couldn't have gotten far in the time it took the lights to come on."

He was right and I knew it. Still, worried as I was about Acacia, I didn't particularly want to go tell the Old Man I'd lost the unknown I was supposed to be escorting. Sure, it probably wasn't *that* big a deal, but . . . "You need any help?" I asked Joaquim, who was still cleaning breakfast off his shirt. He glanced at Jerzy, who gave me a look that said he knew I was trying to stall and he wasn't going to let me. I stuck my tongue out at him. "You're not an officer yet," I teased.

It didn't take long to get to the Old Man's office; I deemed it imperative enough that I hopped on a few conveyers to get me there. Sooner than I'd have liked, I was standing in front of his desk, watching him shuffle through papers like he had far more important things to concern himself with.

"Sir?" I wasn't sure he'd heard me the first time. He glanced up at me, his bionic eye spearing me like a proverbial deer in the headlights. I gathered my nerve, then spoke again. "Acacia Jones disappeared after the punch. She seemed to be in some distress, sir."

"I heard you, and I nodded. The nod meant 'I heard you.' Is there anything else?"

I took a breath. "I . . . shouldn't we be . . . concerned? Sir?"

He set down the stack of papers on his desk with enough force that my hair shifted slightly from the wind. "No, Harker, we should not. Do you recall when your mud-luff companion went AWOL after appearing in the Hazard

Zone?" I nodded. "Some things are not compatible with other things. That's all there is to it." He waited a moment to see if I was stupid enough to say something else. I almost was, but he continued before my brain got quite that far. "I suggest you go take some leisure time. There will be a training exercise later."

I was still almost stupid enough to press the point, but the Old Man's intercom blipped and his assistant's voice filled the room. "Jayarre to see you, Captain."

"Send him in." The Old Man didn't take his eyes off me. I swallowed what I'd wanted to say, stepping out of his office. I passed Jayarre—who gave me a tip of his top hat on his way in—and Josetta, who was still listening to the Old Man through the com. "—Joryn, Jirathe, Jyelda, Jeric, and J'emi," he was saying, while Josetta took notes. All officers. "And get me Jaroux," I heard as I stepped into the hallway, which gave me pause. He was gathering up a bunch of officers—but why the librarian?

There was one whole sector of the ship devoted to nondigital information—books in all shapes and sizes, dictionaries, encyclopedias, magazines, newspapers, printed and bound pages from Wikipedia-esque websites on various worlds—the list went on. The library sector was where we got our study books for various classes, though Jaroux was the strictest librarian I'd ever met. He had a quirky sense of humor and would happily chat for hours on any subject, but no excuse on any ten worlds would help you if you returned a book late—or worse, damaged.

A plan was forming in my head. I had the next few hours off, and had been encouraged to take some leisure time. The library sector was a great place to do just that—and I was perfectly aware that in addition to an extensive cross-referencing system, the library had a full set of census reports from nearly every world we had access to for the past hundred years, some of them organized by person.

It was a start.

Soon after Jaroux had whistled his cheerful way down the hall toward the Old Man's office, I slipped around and through the doors. I didn't have to sneak, really; we had access to the library at all times, even if Jaroux was out. "Knowledge is free," he'd said more than once, "and should always be available even if I'm not." He was also quick to remind us that he knew every single item in there personally, and would know if something went missing. Most of us suspected it was just because each book had a tracer in it.

I didn't plan on checking out a book, but I didn't have to worry about explaining why I was suddenly interested in a century's worth of census reports.

Truth to tell, I wasn't all that sure why. I just *knew* I wasn't being told the whole story, or anything close to it, about the mysterious Ms. Jones. After all, trying to get a straight answer from her was like pulling shark's teeth. Which I didn't mind, really; in fact, I kind of respected it. Despite her "grandma's steamer trunk" fashion sense, it seemed obvious to me that she was in some form of military or paramilitary organization. The swift and smooth way that she'd extracted us from our initial fracas on F∆98[6] would be proof enough of that; plus there was the grudging but unmistakable respect that the Old Man accorded her. Add to that the mysterious lack of concern he'd shown when I told him she'd vanished during the punch, and there was more than met the sensory organs here.

And even aside from all *that*, I'd seen her expression pretty clearly right before she'd vanished. She'd been more than disoriented, she'd been afraid.

"Search people, name: Acacia Jones," I told the catalog, which immediately brightened and made a faint whirring noise.

"Search complete. Four trillion, seven billion, thirty-six million, nine thousand, seven hundred, and fifty-eight matches."

I stared at it, dumbfounded. Was that normal? I'd never done a name search before.

"Search people, name: Joseph Harker," I said, just to be sure.

"Search complete. Three thousand, eight hundred, and twenty-three matches."

That was a slightly more manageable number, considering that "Joseph Harker" was a fairly common name, I *knew* there were several different versions of me with the same name spread throughout the Altiverse, and I was searching census records for the last hundred years.

I stared at the machine for a moment longer. "Search people, name: Acacia Jones. Parameters: age fourteen to sixteen, hair color black, eye color violet."

The whirring noise again, then: "Search complete. Four trillion, seven billion, thirty-six million, six thousand, seven hundred, and three matches."

It wasn't possible. Narrowing the search had only eliminated three thousand, fifty-five people? *Every single other mention* of Acacia Jones in the Altiverse was between fourteen and sixteen with black hair and *violet eyes*? More than four trillion of them?

I didn't even know what to do next. Finally, at a loss, I asked which section contained the first thousand records.

Not all of them were Acacia, as roughly half of the stat sheets contained both a DOB and DOD. I wasn't sure if I was comforted by this or not, although it did make things go a little faster once I narrowed the search to include only living organisms. Finally, after almost two hours of numbly flipping pages, one of the sheets included something new: an affiliation category, which listed the letters *TW*.

All the other stats on the sheet seemed to match up.

Just to be sure, I flipped through a few more. The ones that seemed likely to be the Acacia I knew all also had the *TW* affiliation.

"Search organizations, initials: *TW*," I told the catalog, after putting the census files away.

"Search complete. Number incalculable." I should have seen that coming.

I tried several different searches, most of them based on the specific worlds which had mentioned Acacia Jones. I tried searching brane by brane, world by world. Some yielded actual numbers but nothing helpful. Half an hour later, I'd gotten nowhere but frustrated.

Too many landscapes, by far . . . even weeding out only the relatively few parallel worlds that contained consciousness—the ones without tended to self-destruct in big rips or cosmological inversions or, worst of all, time loops that consisted of a few seconds to a few millennia after each big bang, only to reset and start all over again. Even, as I said, not counting all the other worlds, which was a number guaranteed to give me and my descendants unto the umpteenth generation myopia and migraines, I still couldn't make a dent in the pile in my lifetime.

Resisting the urge to pound my forehead against the screen and apply several of the juicier phrases and words I'd picked up from Jai's unabridged, I instead closed my eyes and counted to ten. I only got to four before I found myself infuriated by the numbers. I was tired of numbers. There were too many freaking numbers.

I took a deep breath. How did you search for one thing that existed *everywhere*?

"Search organizations, initials: *IW*."

"Search complete. Number incalculable."

Wait a minute. InterWorld existed *everywhere*, didn't it?

"Search organizations, name: InterWorld."

"Search complete. One match." The information came up on the screen, listing Joseph Harker as captain and some of the higher-level officers.

I felt myself on the verge of some sort of breakthrough, but I wasn't sure what. Maybe I was just grasping at straws, but this train of thought seemed to be going *somewhere*. If I was searching for something that might exist *everywhere*—

Bingo.

"Search organizations, initials: *TW*. Location: Altiverse."

"Search complete. One match."

The information sheet came up on the screen—and then, like one of those infuriating game demos that made you pay money before you saw the whole thing, the screen dimmed and a message popped up: OFFICER CLEARANCE REQUIRED.

I obviously didn't have officer clearance, nor was it likely I could get it. I'd spent the last several hours going through records, and for all my searching, I'd gotten one word.

One word, barely visible, nearly hidden behind that

smug OFFICER CLEARANCE notice.

TimeWatch.

It wasn't that I was snooping, I told myself for the hundredth time, so much as pursuing knowledge. That was a worthy cause, right? The Old Man always said to learn everything you could, because you never knew when one little piece of information could be important.

I doubted he would take that as a valid excuse if he found me going through his desk like this, but I was driven by a deep, gut-wrenching sense that this was *important*. I had to know.

After standing there with my nose pressed to the monitor for a few minutes, trying in vain to glean any more information on TimeWatch through the dimmed screen and large letters demanding clearance, I'd made my way back to the Old Man's office, intent on asking him about it. Or asking for clearance. Or asking for temporary clearance for something completely unrelated and then using it to get information about TimeWatch. The latter had seemed to be my best option, but all plans had been foiled when Josetta informed me that Captain Harker wasn't in his office.

I'd agreed to wait, sinking into one of the surprisingly plush chairs opposite her desk, and had proceeded to work myself into a frenzy of speculation while she sat there calmly, filing papers.

Four trillion, seven billion, thirty-six million, nine thousand, seven hundred, and fifty-eight matches. The familiar voice of the computer kept running through my head: the same female voice that asked for identification in some doorways, informed us of routine schedule changes or to get ready for a warp, answered questions in the viewing room, and gave instructions in the port room. Being used to it didn't make it any less maddening, especially when it was telling me I didn't have clearance. This information could help me find out where Acacia had gone, if she was okay. *I had to know.*

After a while, Josetta had gotten up to use the lavatory. Before I even knew what I was doing I was in the Old Man's office, opening one of his drawers. He had temporary clearance cards in there; I'd seen him give one to J/O before, which had rankled something awful at the time. They were one-shots, but it just might give me the boost I needed to find out what TimeWatch was.

Index cards, pens, staples, several pocket references on every subject imaginable, a calculator that looked like it could decipher string theory and give it to you in simple terms, two portable intercoms, a gun that probably shot something nastier than bullets—no clearance cards. I was already inventing all the different ways he could kill me if he found me in here. Maybe they were further in the back.

I pulled the drawer out more, finding a few more reference books, personal notebooks, and something that stopped me dead the moment I saw it.

It was a photo, old, scratched, and worn; it looked like it might have survived a fire at one point and possibly a flood. Despite the poor quality, the people were unmistakable. After all, you always recognize yourself in photos, even if that self is a few decades older.

The Old Man wasn't so old in it, and he still had both eyes. He was wearing blue jeans and a loose white tank top that looked like it had seen better days, an army jacket of some kind tucked under his arm. Tucked under his other arm was a girl who *was* older than I was used to seeing, her wicked grin as unmistakable as the green circuitry nail that was visible as she gave the photographer a thumbs-up.

Acacia Jones, plus about ten years. With the Old Man.

CHAPTER NINE

I DON'T KNOW HOW long I would have stood there, dumbfounded, if the loudspeaker hadn't pinged. I just about jumped out of my skin at the Old Man's voice, but logic kicked in a second later to assure me that if he was over the loudspeaker, it meant he was stationary—not on his way back to the office, where he would catch and inevitably kill me.

"All junior Walkers, report to the assembly hall. As some of you know, classes are suspended today in lieu of a little exercise. Team assignments are already posted." Since he was still on the loudspeaker, I had a few more precious seconds while he spoke.

Trying to calm my racing heart, I looked back down at the photograph. It was *definitely* the Old Man and definitely Acacia. I turned it over in my hand—and almost jumped out of my skin again, dropping it back into the drawer. The back of the photograph didn't have a date, or any kind of label, just scrawled words: *Put it back.*

"Excuse me." Josetta's sharp, firm voice came right on the tail end of the Old Man's announcement. I was profoundly grateful at my own jumpiness; I'd slammed the drawer shut the second I heard the door, so it's not like I'd just been caught red-handed or anything. I wasn't even standing behind the Old Man's desk, I was standing next to it. I might be able to play this off.

"Sorry," I apologized, trying to call up the same tone I'd mastered when Mom would catch me hovering *near* the cookie jar. "I figured if he was by a telecom, I could just ping him real fast and ask my question."

Josetta looked at me calculatingly, but she could see my empty hands were nowhere near the desk and my clothing wasn't baggy enough to conceal anything. She relaxed a hair as I adopted a chagrined expression, as though I'd only just realized how incriminating this looked. "Sorry," I said again.

"You'd better get down there," she said with a smile, and then, in the exact same tone, "and don't take this personally." She stepped forward and searched me. I was momentarily glad I hadn't found the clearance cards.

"Nothing personal," she repeated, after failing to find anything incriminating on me. I nodded, still adopting what I hoped was an embarrassed smile. "Go on, now."

I left, my nerves rattling around in my stomach. That

had been stupid; if she'd caught me stealing a clearance card, I would have been in serious trouble. I'd already been kicked out once; I was willing to bet that if I made trouble again, it would be bye-bye, Joey, no questions asked.

And it wasn't like I'd come away empty-handed, figuratively speaking, at least. The Old Man knew Acacia. Or an older version of her. But with four *trillion* para-incarnations of her in the Altiverse, that likely didn't mean much. So he knew an older version of her, or would, in the future. Was Time-Watch like InterWorld—an organization made up of Acacias instead of Joeys? That seemed the most likely explanation, but why were there so many *more* of her than there were of me? And why weren't we already working with them?

Despite the fact that I now knew the Old Man had some kind of connection with Acacia, I wasn't sure how much that would help me. Could I actually ask him about it? There was no way I could admit to snooping around in his desk. I could lie and say I'd found some relevant information in the census files, but he likely knew exactly what kind of clearance could get you what information.

I was still musing when I entered the assembly hall a few minutes later, and the sudden onslaught of noise disoriented me for a moment. I'd spent the last few hours sitting in the library wing with only the computer for company, and now I was abruptly in a room with a few hundred other Walkers, all still talking about the punch this morning and the mysterious new Walker Joeb's team had brought back. I also heard the name "Joaquim" at least a dozen times as I went through the room. I was headed specifically for Jo's white wings, which were easily visible among my mostly redheaded para-incarnations.

"Hey," I said as I got closer, also discovering Jai and J/O. "You feeling better?"

"All systems operational," said J/O.

"Well, that's good. But how are you *feeling*?"

He just looked at me, for long enough that the silence got a little awkward. What was that all about? J/O wasn't *all* computer—he'd answered questions like that before with no issue. "Fine," he said, and then I was distracted by another voice to my side.

"J/O's recovery was much swifter than initially anticipated," Jai said, giving his signature peaceful smile. "And the doctors pronounced him fit enough to participate in our assignment."

"Glad to see you awake," I told him. Honestly, the sudden reunion with my team made me feel a little guilty. I'd been so caught up with Acacia and the archives and my attempted theft that I hadn't really thought about the fact that I'd last seen two of them unconscious in the infirmary.

Jai smiled again, and looked like he was about to say something regarding our mutual idiocy in leaving the link open while expending a large amount of power (except he would have used more syllables), but a hush fell over the room just then, and we knew what that meant.

The Old Man walked out into the front of the room, commanding silence just by his presence, as usual. The noise dulled to a low murmur before he'd even stopped walking, and by the time he'd turned to face us, you could have heard a pin drop on the next planet over.

"This evening's mission is, much like the others you've experienced, a search-and-retrieve scenario." I tried to quench the feeling of dread in my gut. Sure, I'd been on other missions since the disastrous HEX incident where my entire team had been captured and I'd been kicked out of Inter-World without so much as a memory, but I could never quite control the fear the words "search and retrieve" stirred in me.

"You're not going far. This exercise will be taking place just beneath us, on our home planet. Your officers have all been equipped with what I like to call hot-cold devices; they will direct you to your goal." That made me feel slightly better. "This mission is a capture-the-flag run, and you will be competing against other teams to retrieve your objective. You may attempt to sabotage one another, and friendly rivalry is encouraged—but do remember we are all ultimately on the same side and any actual injuries will be investigated *thoroughly*." He paused a moment to let that sink in, his bionic eye roaming over each and every one of us. "The matchups will follow on the screen, in the order of departure; we'll be sending you down to your designated areas one team at a time. Once you see your name, proceed to the port room. You have an hour from the time you land to return with your flag. Good luck."

He turned to leave, and I realized I hadn't really been listening. Running over the conversation in my mind, I found I'd retained the information—but I'd been trying to see through his stern demeanor to the expression he'd worn in the picture with Acacia. I'd been trying to find *that* man beneath the brusque, soldier-like attitude of Captain Harker. It hadn't been easy, but I thought there'd been a hint of it when he'd said "good luck," in the way his eyebrows had relaxed a moment and the corners of his mouth had almost turned up. It was something.

"Any idea who we'll be up against?" I asked as we turned to the screen, receiving only a shrug from Jo and nothing at all from J/O. I was starting to wonder if he had a problem with me again. We'd mostly gotten over our enmity months ago, as far as I was concerned, but now he was acting all aloof.

"I imagine we'll find out for certain upon reading the notice; there's little point in conjecture."

"What he said," agreed Josef as he ambled over. Jakon was with him.

So we were all together again, and none the worse for wear. "How'd your reports go?" I asked, keeping one eye on the screen as it listed team assignments.

They all made general nods or noises of the "fine" variation, except J/O. I was all set to get irritated at him for being sullen when he spoke up.

"I didn't have to make a report, since they just recorded from my memory banks." He sounded smug. I was *definitely* going to have to watch my temper with him right now.

"Well, good on you," Jakon commented, and I could tell she was a little miffed by his attitude, too. Josef glanced at me.

"Heard you got in trouble with Jernan."

I made a face. "Yeah. He was pretty pissed at me for losing a disk." I glanced at Jo. "Don't suppose you'd be willing to tell him I was trying to save your life?"

Jo shook her head. "You're on your own," she said, though she was smiling.

"You're all very supportive," I told my team.

"There we are." Josef pointed to the screen, which had all of our names down one column and six names listed opposite us. I perked up a little; it was Jerzy's team. The quick-witted bird boy had been one of the first people I'd actually gotten along with here, before we'd officially been assigned to teams.

"We're against Joliette." Jakon glanced at Jo, who looked annoyed. Joliette, while not an *actual* vampire, was nevertheless the closest thing most of us had ever encountered. She had pointed canines and pale skin, and while she didn't bite necks or have an aversion to crosses, blood was a healthy part of her diet. As vampires had actually existed in the world Jo came from, Jo and Joliette had a mostly friendly rivalry going. The rest of us were amused at the dichotomy: Jo's white wings made her look angelic, while Joliette had a darker persona, and we liked to pit them against each other whenever possible.

"And Jenoh," Jo retorted. Jakon bared her teeth excitedly. Jenoh was more catlike than wolfish, but the two had a friendly rivalry, as well. I wondered if the Old Man had set us against this team on purpose; I wouldn't have put it past him.

I looked back to the screen. It was us versus Jerzy, Joliette, Jaya, Jenoh, Jorensen, and—

"Afternoon, rivals-to-be." Joaquim gave us a small smile as he wandered over, Joliette beside him. "Anything in particular I should know about this?"

"You're gonna lose," I teased him.

"We'll see," said Joliette, before Joaquim could say anything. "Hey, Jo. How's the wing?"

"Fine, except I can't fly and it hurts."

"Guess we're all on even ground, then."

I glanced at Jo. Despite her quick retorts, she seemed . . . off. Her tone was a little duller, her wings drooping, her skin a shade paler. I worried for about half a second, then realized they wouldn't have let her out of the infirmary if she wasn't up to this. And speaking of being up to this . . .

"They're sending you out already?" I asked Joaquim. "I was in training for weeks before I even left Base."

"I was sitting in that room for hours before you guys found me. Gave me some time to get used to the whole thing, and, believe me, I'd rather be here than there. I want to get started," he said, looking uncomfortable but determined. "I want to start helping."

"I know the feeling," said Jerzy, who'd just woven through the crowd to stand beside us. "I couldn't wait to get out on my first mission after I was picked up by InterWorld."

Jorensen nodded at Jai, who gave his own nod of greeting back. They were the two senior Walkers on this mission, which struck me as somewhat funny; Jorensen was as taciturn as Jai was verbose.

"Where's Hue?"

I turned to see Jenoh, who was smiling at me in a manner both cute and feral. While most of the Walkers viewed Hue with uncertainty or suspicion, some had made friends with him. Jenoh was one of them, though I suspected it was mostly due to her catlike nature and Hue's occasional resemblance to a ball of string.

"Dunno," I said. "He pops in and out. Haven't seen him since last night."

Jenoh pouted cutely and made a noncommittal sound of acceptance. We were almost to the port room now, and more of Jorensen's group was falling in with us. Soon the only one missing was Jaya, who showed up right as we reached the door.

"Hey," I greeted her. She gave a sweet smile in return, her red-gold hair falling over her shoulders in waves.

"Hey, Joey." Her voice sounded a lot like mine, as everyone's did, but far more melodic—it had such a sweet tone to it that I didn't mind the nickname. "Do we have everyone, Jorensen?" The officer gave a nod, gesturing for his team to step sideways, over by one of the doors.

They all filed over, as the team before us vanished through the port. "Proceed through in single file," said the familiar ship voice, "and please watch your step."

"We'll give you a head start," I tossed out, earning a snort from Jerzy and a grateful glance from Joaquim before he realized I was kidding.

"We won't need it," Jorensen's deep, good-natured voice came from next to me. I was glad I wasn't the only one participating in the banter.

Jorensen's team went through, single file as instructed, then it was our turn. "Get ready, guys," I told my team. "Once we go out there, all bets are off."

They nodded, and I stepped through.

Going through a port is kind of like misjudging how many steps there are before you reach the bottom. You start to bring your foot down, ready to take another step, and the ground meets you just a little bit sooner than you expect. No matter how careful you are, it sends a jolt up your leg, sometimes rattling your teeth. It's even more unnerving because you're never exactly sure *where* you're stepping, since you can't see the ground.

This time the jolt wasn't as bad, though that was just because my foot landed in a muddy puddle about three inches deep. We'd ported into the middle of a lush, green forest, and it looked like it had just rained. "Mud," I cautioned, turning to the others as they appeared behind me. "All right, Jai. Where're we going?"

"Down!" he yelled, and I immediately obliged. When Jai only uses one syllable, it's serious. Something hurtled over my head, and as I rolled to my feet, getting mud all over me, I realized it was Jenoh. It was my turn to yell.

"What's the big idea?"

"We're allowed to sabotage each other, remember?" she responded sweetly, already back in pouncing position. She and Jakon squared off, a growl starting in the wolf girl's throat.

I looked at Jai, who nodded to the left of me. Okay, then, left it was. I made eye contact with the rest of my team, except for Jakon, and we all took off before Jenoh could try to stop us again. We sprinted through the trees, occasionally squelching in pockets of mud, the mostly playful growls and hisses of Jenoh and Jakon fading behind us.

"J/O, scan for the others!" I half expected him to protest or ignore me, but the bionic boy gave a nod and fixed his cybernetic gaze on the scenery around us.

"Joliette is up ahead, twenty yards northeast."

"Jo, you want her?" The winged girl nodded, splitting off from us to come from a different angle. I was willing to bet she wouldn't have cared had Joliette not made the comment about her wing earlier.

"How far are we from the flag, Jai?"

"The device does not indicate precise proximity."

"Just direction?"

"Affirmative."

I squinted off into the distance. Through the trees, I could see the sky, the clouds, the sparkle of something that may have been a lake but could just be an optical illusion, and the top of what looked like a very tall mountain.

"I bet it's up there," I said as we paused near the edge of the tree line. Jai squinted as well.

"You may be correct."

"There's Jerzy!" Josef pointed. About a hundred yards from us, Jerzy's bright red feather tips were visible against the lush green grass.

"I love that guy's head," I said, which made Jai laugh.

"It does enable us to locate him more easily in this locale," he agreed.

"Let's go," Josef said eagerly, but I paused.

"I bet they've got something planned. If we run out there, we're gonna get ambushed. Jai, can I have the locator?" He handed it to me, looking curious.

"Can you do your 'we're not here' trick on us when we break cover?" He hesitated, then nodded. I knew it was difficult to do on moving targets, but there were only three of us. "You don't have to hold it for long. Just give us a start toward the mountain." The little disk was warm in my hand; I felt fairly confident that the mountain was, in fact, where we needed to go.

Jai took a breath, then closed his eyes and motioned to the air around us. "Proceed."

We broke from the trees, Josef, J/O, and I, running for all we were worth for the base of the mountain. The back of my neck tingled; I expected something to attack me at any moment, but it was the fun kind of adrenaline, like when you're a kid sneaking around playing hide-and-seek.

An energy pulse hit the ground a few feet away from us; someone was using a blaster gun on stun. We were out in the middle of the plain—there was nowhere to hide, which probably meant they also had an invisi-shield up. I berated myself for not thinking to snag some helpful gadgets on the way out, then remembered Jernan, the quartermaster, was still mad at me and I likely would have been out of luck anyway. Somehow, that made me feel better about my lack of foresight.

Jorensen was revealed a second later, which meant Jai had discovered him and fritzed his invisi-shield—which also meant he'd dropped our "we're not here" spell. I could still see Jerzy headed for the mountain off in the distance, but Joaquim and Jaya were still unaccounted for.

"J/O, you sense anything?"

"Jakon's caught up with Jo, and Joliette's on her way back."

"That's great, but do you sense anything *up ahead*?" He turned his attention to the terrain in front of us as we ran. I didn't know why he'd even been bothering to look behind us in the first place.

Jakon must have beat Jenoh, but Joliette was on her way back? Jo didn't usually lose to her. She'd been at InterWorld longer and was quicker in a fight. She *had* seemed a little low energy, though. I wondered if she was on pain medication for her wing.

"No," J/O answered simply, and if I hadn't been trying to conserve breath at that point I might have told him he could stand to be a little more helpful.

We were almost to the rocks now, but I'd lost sight of Jerzy. It was harder to see him against the brown stone, especially with the sun setting behind us and casting a bright red light over everything. The little disk in my hand was pulsing steady warmth—we were definitely getting closer.

"This was actually pretty straightforward," I commented to my team as we reached the base of the mountain.

"I think the real challenge is getting *up* there," Josef rumbled. J/O didn't say anything.

I stood with my back to Josef, keeping an eye out for Jerzy, Joaquim, or Jaya. Or Joliette, for that matter, since I didn't know how long it would take her to get here.

"Well, at least we know none of them can fly up."

"Neither can any of us, with Jo's wing busted."

"Yeah," I agreed, and then I had an idea. "Jai can hover. If he makes himself light, can you throw him?" Josef nodded. "That'd get us a head start, at least. Jakon's a climber, too. Throw her and Jai up, when they get here. As high as you can. J/O and I will start climbing."

Josef nodded again, seeming perfectly happy to *not* climb the mountain himself. He was a pretty big, heavy guy, and I bet he didn't relish the thought of finding out which rocks were loose the hard way.

"C'mon, J/O!" I tried for cheerful, but I was still getting a wall where there used to be a person. I wondered if he was mad at me.

"You come on," he retorted. "You know I can outclimb you." That was a little more like his usual, competitive self, but I still had the feeling something was off with him.

"Hey, is there a problem?" I asked as soon as we were out of earshot of Josef. The mountain had something akin to a trail for the first few steps, but after those first few, it was a matter of scrambling up over rocks to various naturally formed platforms that were getting both smaller and steeper.

"No." J/O looked at me oddly, sidelong. "Why would there be?"

I didn't get a chance to respond, since he abruptly turned his head to look up the mountain. "Jaya is ahead," he informed me.

"Huh. Why don't you go first. You're immune to her siren trick, aren't you?" He nodded, and continued to climb without another word. I waited until I heard Jaya's voice, singing the first few notes of the most beautiful song I'd ever heard—anything Jaya sang would make you think that—and then silence. I was far enough away that it didn't affect me *too* much, but I was still sorry to hear it stop.

I started climbing again, feeling the little disk in my pocket pulse faster. I was nowhere near the top yet, but it looked like there were some caves scattered around the outside. Instead of being at the very top, the flag could be hidden in one of those.

I considered a moment; I didn't want to give away my position, but J/O had already neutralized Jaya—how, I wasn't sure, but she'd obviously stopped singing—and he didn't know where the flag was. "J/O?" I called. Silence.

I pulled myself up onto a large, mostly flat rock. I'd been right: There was a small cave, not much bigger than I was, nestled between two rocks. I could see from where I stood that it was empty, but a natural path wound up around it off to the right, looking like it could take me higher. I started forward—and my senses screamed at me to *duck*. Jerzy's slow kick whooshed over my head as he stepped out from behind an outcropping of rock.

"Took you long enough." His hair feathers ruffled as he settled back into a defensive stance.

"I said we'd give you a head start," I retorted, lashing out with a fist. He dodged easily, dancing around in a semicircle.

I bounced a little on my toes, adrenaline starting to pump through me. I'd always enjoyed sparring with Jerzy; he was light and quick, about my size, and always had a retort or comeback ready with his punches. He didn't take things personally, he just enjoyed the test of strength and ability.

"You sent the new kid to get the flag for you?" I teased, ducking under another kick and crouching to sweep him.

"His idea." Jerzy jumped agilely, landing slightly to my left. "Pretty eager to prove himself since he had to be rescued, I think. Reminds me of someone . . ."

"Hey, I did my fair share of rescuing in the end." I dodged, blocked, struck, dodged, and blocked again as Jerzy put me on the defensive, finally ducking out of the way as I felt the rock wall at my back.

"*After* you got kicked out," he teased me. I didn't mind, especially because I got a shot in at that moment: a solid punch to the jaw. Jerzy shook his head and laughed, bringing a knee up into my side. We were pulling our blows some, but it still hurt. I laughed, rolling away from him.

"Yeah, and I was back within a week. I'd have that flag by now, too—he's slow."

Jerzy danced back at that, glancing up toward the mountain. I didn't press the advantage; a slight frown crossed his face at my comment, and he lowered his guard a little. "I believe that, actually. Hey, Joaquim!" he called up, cupping one hand around his mouth. "Hurry up! They're coming!"

I turned to glance over my shoulder at that; Jerzy was on a slightly higher vantage point than I was, and had seen the rest of my team before I did. Joliette was climbing up the way I'd come, Jo not far behind her, and Jai was making his way toward the mountain while the air around him rippled as Jorensen's stunner pinged off the force field. Josef waved at me, then boosted Jakon up onto the mountain one-handed, The other hand was holding a struggling, hissing Jenoh aloft by the back of her shirt.

"My team's here," I tossed back at Jerzy.

He turned to look at me, that frown still on his face. He opened his mouth—and something exploded.

We both looked up at the same time, as another explosion went off, then another—a series of small pops sounding almost like fireworks, one after the other. There were five or six of them total, but the popping was soon replaced by a rumbling, and it began to rain pebbles and dust.

"What's—" I started, but I couldn't even hear myself over the sound of falling rocks. I stared up at the cloud of dust and earth, thoughts going through me as calmly as if it were happening to someone else. *Avalanche. There's nowhere to go, no cover. The mountainside won't protect us, and we're too far up to jump. Those rocks are huge—*

Jerzy moved first, launching himself toward me and tugging me over to the edge. Jumping was our only option—

The cave. I planted my feet, tugging back on Jerzy's arm. A boulder the size of my dad's car slammed into the rock we stood on, splitting it in two. I stumbled sideways, losing my grip on Jerzy. I couldn't see anything—the dust in the air was so thick now I couldn't breathe, but I stubbornly forced my eyes open, trying to find him, to pull him toward the cave.

Another rock fell just beside me, clipping my left shoulder on the way down. It hurt like *hell*, and I stumbled back—just in time, as another one landed where I'd been standing. I just kept backpedaling, instinct taking over as it grew darker; the avalanche was literally blocking out the sun.

Not even able to keep my feet anymore, I scrambled backward until I felt the rocks at my side, felt along them until I found the depression of the cave. I crawled into it, praying I'd find Jerzy already there.

I didn't. Then a noise almost too loud to comprehend sounded just next to me, the world lurched, and I fell.

I remember hearing voices sometime after that, though I didn't know whose they were. I remember being aware of total darkness, then it got a little brighter, like a light turning on while your eyes are still closed. I remember feeling *wrong*, like when you fall asleep in a place you're not used to and don't know where you are upon waking up.

I thought I heard crying, and I know I felt a hand grab my wrist. I heard strong, no-nonsense commands from a voice that sounded like my dad, and someone was asking me questions.

I couldn't breathe, and I couldn't see, and I think I was trying to say something but I don't know if it was coming out right. I had to tell them Jerzy hadn't made it to the flag. I had to tell them he would have won, if I hadn't pulled him toward the cave. I had to tell them what I'd seen before the rocks fell, but I wasn't sure I remembered what it was anymore.

". . . crippled," someone was saying, "but it's not likely. . . . Several broken bones, multiple contusions, and thirteen stitches, but stable."

"This one?"

"Cracked collarbone and dislocated jaw, sprained wrist."

"This one." The voice was emotionless and methodical. It didn't sound like my dad anymore.

"Compound fracture of the radius, three broken fingers, eleven stitches, twisted ankle."

Footsteps sounded across the room from me, then the voice again. "Him?" The voice sounded muffled, like the person was facing away from me.

"Bruising. Dehydration and exhaustion. He passed out from the energy expended to shield them."

This place smelled familiar. The air was sharp and tangy but somehow still. It smelled like medicine. . . . I was in the infirmary.

"This one."

"Proximal humerus fracture, bruised ribs, dust inhalation. The cave protected him from the worst of it."

That had to be me. I tried to move, to show I was awake and see how everyone else was, but my body wasn't responding to the urges of my brain.

"Not an uninjured one in the whole lot, but only one casualty."

"One too many," the older voice said roughly, and I stopped struggling to move. The words rang in my head louder than anything I'd ever heard, and seeing as I'd just survived a rockslide, that said a lot. *One casualty.* I managed to ease my eyes open, then squeezed them closed again. They burned and my eyelids felt like sandpaper, but I stubbornly kept at it, blinking to clear my vision. I tried to lift my hand to rub them, and the pain made tears well up. Though they hurt, the tears actually helped, and after blinking a few more times I could see the bright white room and the beds opposite and around me.

As before, Jai was across from me and Jo was next to me,

both asleep or unconscious. Jorensen was in the bed to one side of me, and the large form in the bed next to Jai could only be Josef. Wavy, golden-red hair spilled over one pillow—Jaya.

I looked around with as much effort as I could muster, identifying everyone I could. Joaquim's darker red hair was visible from a bed near the door. J/O looked unharmed, powered down and seated in a chair nearby.

I struggled to sit, ignoring the voices telling me to be still as I continued to look around the room. I saw the tip of Jenoh's tail and Joliette's pale skin, one of Jakon's lightly furred, clawed hands with splints on three of her fingers, but nowhere in the stark white room did I see the bright red feather tips of Jerzy's hair.

CHAPTER TEN

THE FUNERAL WAS A lot like Jay's had been, except I saw it from the front row instead of the infirmary window. I was between Jo and Josef, the only two on my team aside from me who were able to stand. Jai was still unconscious, the least of Jakon's injuries was a twisted ankle, and J/O was still powered down. He'd been close enough to the explosions that some of his circuitry had been fried. He'd survive, they were pretty sure. They just didn't know if he'd be fully functional.

The Old Man stood on the platform in front of a coffin, talking about when Jerzy had first come to InterWorld. He told a brief story about how Jerzy's enthusiasm for training had gotten him locked in the Hazard Zone overnight once, and some of us laughed. Jo was crying. So was I.

I'd wondered, at the time, where Jay's body had gone when he'd died. The box had shimmered and vanished, but

I didn't know where to. In a few moments, the same thing would happen to Jerzy. I wished I could see his bright red hair feathers one more time, but the coffin was closed. He'd been so buried in the avalanche that one of the rocks had crushed his chest, and the Old Man hadn't wanted any of us to see him like that. When he'd said so, I'd looked again in his expression for the man he'd been in the picture with Acacia. I couldn't see it, this time. That man had been happy. This one just looked tired.

I understood the shouting now, too. It was the first thing I'd seen at Jay's funeral, when I'd watched from the infirmary; as the coffin vanished, five hundred people lent their voices to a single shout, a last hurrah. I hadn't gotten it then, but now even though my ears rang and my throat itched and my eyes stung, I understood the noise as it left my throat. Though I didn't use any words, I was shouting *Look out!* I was shouting *This way, there's a cave.* I was shouting *I'm sorry.* I was saying good-bye. We all were.

The music played and we all stood there as the coffin vanished. Some of us cried. Some of us hugged. I wanted to take Jo's hand, but my arm was in a sling and my shoulder was killing me, and I needed my free hand to wipe my eyes so I could see. I wasn't sure she'd appreciate it, anyway. After all, it was entirely possible I was the one who'd gotten Jerzy killed in the first place.

I'd played the scene over and over in my mind as I recovered in the infirmary after the funeral. I saw it when I dreamed, and I remembered everything about it I could when I was questioned. He'd pulled me to the edge so we could try to jump. I'd remembered the cave, and pulled him back. A rock had hit my shoulder, and I'd felt his hand slip from mine. I hadn't been able to see him anymore. Had I tried to call out? I couldn't remember. Maybe if I'd called out, he could have found me. Maybe he'd have been able to make it to the cave.

Classes were scheduled as usual that day; the death of a Walker didn't mean we could take a break. It meant we had to work harder. It meant things had just gotten worse for us. It meant we had one less person standing in the way of HEX and Binary. It meant we all had to band together.

Except me, apparently.

"Joey Harker."

"Sir." My voice sounded dull and flat. I was tired; I hadn't been able to sleep the night after Jerzy's funeral. I kept dreaming he was falling toward me, and if I could just catch him, I could tell everyone he wasn't dead.

"Your injuries should heal in a matter of weeks, three at the most. If you take daily vitamins and refrain from any strenuous activity, you should be well enough to train again in two, maybe even one. See the doctors *every night*. Understood?"

"Yes, sir."

"You've been diagnosed with post-traumatic stress disorder. You understand what that means?"

"Yes, sir."

"Your daily schedule is cleared until further notice. You will be injected with a tracer, for your own safety. Regular sessions with the therapist have been scheduled."

"Yes, sir." My mind was numb. I didn't know what else to say—I was just glad they weren't killing me. Or worse, taking my memories and kicking me out. After all, I knew what the Old Man wasn't saying: I'd now been present for the deaths of *two* Walkers. They'd already taken a chance with me; they couldn't take any more. I wasn't benched because I had PTSD, I was on probation. One wrong move, and I'd be out of here so fast it'd make my head spin, assuming it was still attached to my shoulders.

Even though classes were going on as usual, depression hung like fog over Base Town, like something tangible and oppressive. The Walkers I encountered in the halls didn't meet my eyes, and most of them just stepped aside to let me pass. Everyone's shoulders drooped; everyone walked with their heads down and their feet shuffling, looking tired and upset.

My sling was both a mark of honor and of shame; everyone knew I'd been there. They knew I'd been injured in an accident that had killed a Walker. What they didn't know was that every time someone stepped aside to let me pass first, every time someone nodded as I walked by, I hated myself a little more.

I hadn't been able to save him. I'd been *right there*, and he'd tried to help me and gotten killed. How many more times was a Walker going to die because of me?

It was like when I'd first come to Base Town after Jay's death, but worse. Back then, five hundred people I didn't even know had hated and shunned me. Now, five hundred *comrades* were looking at me askance.

I wouldn't have gone so far as to call all of them friends. I still didn't know all of them, at least not personally. Living with five hundred or so other people whose names all started with *J* made it a little hard to get to know everyone, but at least I'd started to fit in. I'd been just another recruit, aside from my friendship with Hue.

Now, the quiet chatter got even quieter as I walked into the mess hall, people lowering their voices or trailing off as they glanced my way. I tried to ignore it, just going over to the cafeteria and getting a tray, but I felt like everyone was watching me. I sat down at an empty table, not even sure if I wanted anyone to come join me. The back of my neck felt prickly, like it had out in the field, but without the pleasant exhilaration. I felt like a mouse in a jar. I missed Jerzy, and I was worried about Acacia and everyone who'd been involved in the avalanche. J/O was still powered down and Jai still hadn't woken up, and it was possible Jorensen would never walk again.

A tray plunked down opposite me, and I looked up to see Joaquim. One side of his face was covered in scratches and abrasions, and he looked as tired as I felt.

"Hey," I offered, trying for a normal tone of voice.

"Hey," he said, and we sat in silence for a while, neither of us eating. "How are you?"

"I've been better."

He glanced at my arm. "Does it hurt?"

"Yeah." I wasn't hungry, but I tried to eat anyway. After a moment, he did the same. "You okay?" I asked him in return.

"Mostly. I . . . No. Not . . ." He looked at the food on his fork, then put it down. "Is it always like this?"

I hesitated. I didn't know how to answer that. No, it wasn't always like this, but . . . when something like this happened, it was always this bad. It was always this hard.

"Losing people is never easy," I said finally.

"I'm sorry," he said. "Is everyone else going to be okay?"

"Yeah. Mostly. Jai and J/O are still unconscious."

He nodded. "Jorensen? He was down at the base when it happened, wasn't he?"

"Yeah. He threw Jenoh into Jai's shield, but couldn't get close enough himself. More than a few broken bones, some stitches. One of his knees is pretty messed up."

"I saw Jo flying right as I fell. She missed the worst of it?"

"She messed up her wing more trying to glide, but I guess

it would have been worse if she hadn't. Have you heard anything else about Jaya?"

We went over it again and again, checking on everyone who'd been involved, exchanging stories. He'd been at the top of the mountain when the rumbling started, he'd said. He'd activated his shield disk and jumped. He asked about everyone still in the infirmary—I was surprised that he knew everyone's name, since he'd just met most of us. He seemed to really be trying to get to know everyone, really trying to fit in. I hadn't tried half as hard when I'd first arrived . . . but then, I'd immediately been ostracized.

"It shouldn't have to be like this," he said suddenly, and something about the way he said it, the conviction in his voice, gave me pause.

"Like what?"

"Like . . . this. We shouldn't have to fight."

"We shouldn't," I agreed. "But we do. If we don't, Binary and HEX will take over. They'll destroy everything, make the Altiverse into what they want."

"A silver dream," he said, turning his fork over in his hands. I wanted to ask what he meant by that, but he continued before I could. "Joey . . . you know a lot of people are blaming you, right?"

"I'm blaming me," I said honestly, and he shook his head.

"Don't. It wasn't your fault. I was there, I know it wasn't. But . . . people are suspicious, anyway." He hesitated, still playing with his fork. "I heard some of the officers talking. . . . They're investigating the possibility of foul play."

I just sat there, letting this run through me. It made sense, of course. How could I not have thought about that? The explosions I'd heard right before the rocks had fallen . . . those hadn't been blasters, and even if they had been, the stun setting didn't sound like that. The Old Man had said any actual injuries would be investigated thoroughly. There'd damn well been some actual injuries, so of *course* they were investigating. And what were they likely to find? Joey Harker, who'd fought with Jerzy right before he'd been killed. Joey Harker, who'd already been accused of selling out his team once. Joey Harker, who'd saved himself and let someone else die.

I'd been pulled out of the avalanche, too, which was probably the only reason I wasn't being treated with outright suspicion, but Joaquim had it right. People *were* suspicious. The sling cradling my arm and healing my fractured shoulder was like my get out of jail free card, except I still wasn't allowed to pass Go or collect any money.

I didn't remember leaving the mess hall, or getting back to my room. I realized at some point that I was sitting on my bed, my shoulder was aching abominably, and the white cloth that held my arm across my chest was splattered with tears. Hue was hovering mournfully beside me.

"Jerzy was my first friend here, aside from you," I told

him. He bobbed sadly, turning a depressed shade of gray blue. I sat in silence for a while longer, before an idea occurred to me and a faint spark of hope flared in my chest. If Hue had been there, maybe he'd seen what had happened. Maybe he'd be able to show the Old Man it had been an accident, not my fault. "Did you see it, Hue? Were you anywhere nearby?" He flickered, giving the impression of a shrug with a well of color that rose to the top of his sphere and faded downward again. I felt the spark of hope do the same within me.

"Where were you?" I asked dully, not really expecting an answer. Or that I'd care for whatever answer he gave. Why did things have to keep going wrong like this?

Hue turned a reddish brown around his lower half, the upper part no single color but a multitude of them, all swirling and blending together.

I didn't understand what he was trying to tell me, and sighed. "Okay," I said, and put my head in one hand. I wasn't tired, but I wanted to be. I wanted to sleep until everything was back to normal again.

The thought tugged a laugh out of me. I remembered when *normal* was going to school and coming home and doing homework, trying to get around doing chores and fighting with my sister over the television. I remembered, with a longing so sharp it hurt, what the dinner table looked like and where everyone sat. I remembered when normal was begging Mom and Dad to let us sit in front of the TV with dinner instead of around that table, and playing video games or messing around on the computer while I ate dessert. I remembered how my room smelled when I was about to fall asleep.

Normal hadn't used to mean morning classes on oscillating solitons and supercontinuums, martial arts after lunch, then Hazard Zone sessions and various taxa of cacodemons before dinner. It hadn't used to mean walking around a corner and running into a mirror, only to have your image excuse himself and step around you. There were some people here who still looked so much like me that I didn't think I'd ever get used to it, no matter how many times I saw them.

They were all me, but none of them seemed to have my luck. None of them seemed to have my penchant for getting into trouble. None of them had seen two of us die.

Hue hovered uncertainly around me for a while, still with that odd multicolored two-tone pattern. I watched him orbit slowly around my head like a planet that's just been kicked out of the solar system, thinking about how Jerzy already had a place on the Wall, and I didn't know what to contribute. Maybe I could do what I'd done for Jay, and get dirt from the base of the mountain. Yeah, that was a great tribute. Dirt that'd had a hand in killing him. Very meaningful.

I sighed, flopping back onto my bed. My shoulder ached at the movement, which only irritated me. No classes, no training, nothing strenuous, and the knowledge that most of my fellow Walkers hated me again. Why was I even here?

Well, it wasn't like I could go anywhere.

Or could I? The Old Man had said I was suspended from classes, not that I couldn't leave the base. And I had a tracker in me, didn't I? Excursions off Base weren't against the rules, as long as you were careful, signed out, and weren't gone for too long. There wasn't anything saying I couldn't just . . . go for a Walk.

That train of thought led to another, and I sat up again after a moment. I knew what to put on Jerzy's Wall.

We'd stepped a few worlds sideways after the accident, from what I was told, to make sure InterWorld stayed hidden. Knowing which Earth to go back to wasn't that difficult; there was a running log of our past locations available to anyone curious enough to look for it, and I had the name in just a few short moments.

I got some odd glances as I went through the locker room, got suited up in basic light armor—just in case—and headed for the hatch. No one stopped me, though; Base was on low-key lockdown, which meant leaving was *discouraged* but not forbidden. I'd signed out, put an estimated time of return, and basically done everything like this was just a normal trip. It *was* just a normal trip. I just . . . wasn't a normal recruit anymore.

I stepped off the ship onto a small mound of sand, flailing my good arm to catch my balance. I hadn't even bothered to ask the quartermaster for a gravity-repulsor disk; he was still mad at me for losing the shield disk, and I wasn't about to push my luck. I was walking.

Well, more specifically, I was Walking, and *then* I was walking. I closed my eyes, took a breath, and followed the threads of a portal into the world I was looking for.

Dust still hung thick in the air near the mountain. I could see it from a distance, a faint miasma that made it almost look like a volcano. I'm sure it didn't need help to look any more ominous, but the debris in the air certainly served to give it a malevolent air. I started toward it, depression settling more heavily over me with every step. I wished I had someone to talk to. I wished I knew where Acacia'd gone, or what Hue had been trying to communicate. I wished I hadn't decided to come back here, even though it would be a fitting tribute for Jerzy.

I walked until I reached the base of the mountain—it was little changed, except for the larger rocks scattered over the ground. I stood still for a moment, just staring up and feeling very small. What looked like only a few rocks out of place had killed a friend of mine and injured two entire teams of combat-trained warriors.

Mother Nature was not something you wanted to mess with.

There were caution markers in certain areas, the kinds we had in some places around Base Town, which usually had motion sensors and cameras in them. Some of the officers were probably intending to sweep the area a few more times. I didn't bother to avoid the cameras as I picked my way through the rocks; they knew I was here already, were probably keeping tabs on me via the tracer, and I wasn't doing anything wrong.

Yes, I'd recognized my need to continually reassure myself, thank you.

I started up the mountain, testing each rock carefully with my foot before putting my weight on it. Some of them shifted even after I'd tested them, sending my heart leaping into my throat and a tremor through my knees every time. Maybe the whole PTSD thing wasn't just an excuse.

It took a fair while for me to get to the top like that, but I didn't dare move any faster. My shoulder was still fractured; I couldn't climb, and I couldn't catch myself if I fell. Every footstep I made sounded like an F-18 crashing to the ground, and there was a little voice in the back of my mind gibbering about how I wouldn't survive a second rockslide. Finally, though, I was standing on a small, natural platform about ten yards below the very top peak.

Some of the boulders up on the plateau with me were blackened and scorched, as was the edge sticking furthest out from the mountain. For a second I was confused; *was* this a volcano? Then I remembered the explosions. Doubtless whoever had been sweeping the area had taken samples to be studied; come to think of it, that was likely why no one was out here now. They may have found all the evidence they needed. I hoped it wouldn't somehow implicate me.

I turned slowly in place, looking for another path up to the peak of the mountain. Instead of finding anything that looked climbable, there was a splash of color against the reddish-brown rocks, half buried against the side of the mountain.

It took some pulling, wriggling and rolling, and more than a few creative swear words, but eventually I stood on the plateau, holding aloft the flag Jerzy had died trying to get.

It wasn't much, as far as tributes went, but I found it oddly fitting. Jerzy had always been so dedicated. He'd said more than once that he owed InterWorld his life, and the best way to pay that back was to dedicate that life to the cause. It infuriated me that he'd died on a *training mission*, of all things. A stupid game of capture the flag. In retrospect, perhaps this wasn't that great a tribute. Maybe I should just leave it here and come up with something else to put on the Wall for him.

I was looking at the flag in disgust, contemplating throwing it over the cliff and Walking home, when a familiar pop sounded just over my right shoulder. Hue bobbed into my line of vision, still sporting the oddly dual-sectioned color scheme he'd had in my room.

"Hey, Hue. I got the flag," I said, surprising myself with the amount of self-mockery in my tone. Hue spun around slowly in place, then bobbed from side to side, trying to tell me something.

I wasn't sure what; my attention was caught by a flash on the ground as the mudluff moved. "Hey, wait, Hue—do that again." He paused, then repeated the motion more slowly, and I located the source of the glint: a transparent bit of what looked like plastic, invisible on the dirt-covered rocks until Hue had passed over it. It must have been dislodged when I'd pulled the flag free.

It looked kind of like those clear plastic circles that come in cases of blank CDs. Or, for those of you who've had extensive schooling in a multidimensional military academy, it looked like an uncharged shield disk.

"Huh." I turned it over in my hands, testing the charge, then the emergency power switch. Nothing worked; it was either completely out of juice or plain broken. I wouldn't know until I could get it back to a charger. I wondered what it was doing there; then I remembered Joaquim's injuries had been mitigated by having a shield disk. I felt a small flare of validation—I wasn't the only one who'd lost a disk, though it'd certainly done Joaquim more good than it had done me. Maybe I could get some points with Jernan by bringing it back.

My shoulders slumped. Jerzy was dead, and I was trying

to think of a way to get the quartermaster to stop being mad at me? I really needed to get my priorities in order.

I turned to Hue. "Ready to go home?"

He bobbed again, that same side-to-side motion. He took on a frustrated grayish red, then returned to the colors he'd had before, the muddy reddish brown on bottom and the swirl of color on top. This time, I really looked.

The colors tugged at a memory—the red, rock-hard dirt where I'd been unable to dig even a shallow grave, and Jay's death beneath that writhing, liquid sky.

"You were back there?" Hue brightened, turning a pleased pink. "What were you doing back there?"

His surface turned reflective, as it had when he'd shown Acacia behind me in my room. Now I saw only my own image, freckles and goofy hair and all, standing dumbly on the mountain with one arm in a sling and a flag in my hand.

"I don't understand." I tried to keep from sounding frustrated, and Hue gave a brief flicker. He pulsed, alternating between the bright, cheerful blue and the reflection, so I was seeing myself every other second. It wasn't particularly helpful.

Perhaps seeing the look of utter perplexity on my face, Hue began to bob back and forth again, floating next to me, then in front of me, alternately reflective and blue depending on where he was. I took a shot in the dark.

"You were interacting with something?" He brightened

so much I almost had to look away, but it made me laugh. I hadn't expected to be right.

"You were talking to someone?" He brightened again. "Do you want me to go there?" He flickered an affirmation, giving a pleased up-and-down bob.

Excited, I rolled up the flag and stuffed it into a pocket, calling to mind the coordinates for the place where I'd first met Hue. Grinning like a fool, I took a step toward the edge, and Walked off the mountain.

There was a lesson here in jumping to conclusions, I was sure, but I didn't really want to think about it.

The planet—or place, or whatever—remained unchanged from the last time I'd seen it, up to and including that swirling sky and the footprints that belonged to Jay and me. There was no wind on this world, apparently, and there were no other footprints—and no other human in sight.

Acacia wasn't here.

I stood for a moment at that point, looking at the larger footsteps that had belonged to Jay. I could still trace where we'd landed, walked a ways, sat and talked, and walked a ways more . . . and where I'd suddenly run off to rescue a creature that I had no reason to believe was friendly. I'd gotten Jay killed by doing that—but I'd gained Hue, who had once rescued me from the clutches of HEX. I still wasn't sure it was a fair trade-off.

"Is it safe here?" I asked Hue, who'd been the captive of a giant monster-dragon-dinosaur-snake-thing—a gyradon, I'd learned later—the last time he'd been here.

"Safe as anywhere, which is relative," my own voice answered.

I looked at Hue, who was bobbing and sporting his *pleased* color. "What?"

The answer was a laugh, one that sounded a lot like mine. "Oh, come on. Figure it out—you're smart enough."

The voice *seemed* to be coming from Hue. I took a few steps, looked around, peered at the little mudluff—nothing. Then, when I took a step sideways, I saw my own face reflected in my balloon-like friend.

No. Not my face.

Jay's.

"Jay!" I spun around, saw nothing, darted behind Hue. Still nothing. That laughter sounded again.

"You've almost got it. Hue, help him out, would you?"

The mudluff circled around me, orienting himself with his "front" to me and his "back" to where the footprints led off—and I could see Jay again, like Hue was some kind of living magnifying glass that didn't actually magnify but let you see things that weren't there.

"I'm looking *through* him," I said out loud, and Jay grinned and nodded.

"Yes."

"But you're . . . really here."

"No, I'm sort of half here. Or I'm here, but I'm sort of half me—it's complicated. Basically, I'm a psychic imprint. I died here, so some of my essence stayed."

"Like a ghost?"

"If you want to call it that. It's close enough, anyway. Not sure if it's more magic or science." He shook his head. "Enough about me. What brings you here?"

"Didn't you? I thought Hue came to get me . . ."

"If he did, it was his idea." Hue gave a pleased flicker, momentarily blocking out Jay's face. "He and I were chatting a little while ago. He apologized for what happened and said he's been doing his best to keep you safe."

"He did?" I tried to alternate between looking at Jay and looking at Hue, but the only way to manage it was to go cross-eyed, and I didn't want Jay to laugh at me again.

"Well, not in so many words. But that was the impression I got."

"Jay . . ." I was having trouble adjusting to the fact that I was standing there *talking to Jay*. I mean, there had been that one time when I'd been falling through the Nowhere-at-All, and Jay's voice had given me advice, but I hadn't been sure if it was really *him* or just *me*. Now, he was standing *right there*. Sort of.

"How're things going at school?" It seemed like an odd question, the kind of thing an older brother would ask when he was trying to break the ice.

It was exactly what I needed. A question I could answer honestly, and someone I could talk to.

I told him everything. I told him about the mission to Earth FΔ98[6] and Joaquim and losing the shield disk and the twin Walkers and the training mission and Jerzy and *everything*—and then I told him about Acacia. Jay just listened, until I recounted my excursion to the library and the paltry results that had yielded. Jay's eyebrows shot up almost to his hairline.

"TimeWatch?" He gave a low whistle.

My heart jumped into my throat. "You know about Time-Watch? What can you tell me?"

Jay hesitated for a moment, considering. "TimeWatch is basically InterWorld, just . . . not yet."

"So . . . they're what InterWorld will become?"

"Not exactly. Look, Joey, I'm not sure how much of this I should tell you."

"Call me Joe. And please, don't do the withholding-information thing. I'm tired of being kept out of the loop for my own good. You died before I even knew what was going on, Jerzy may have just died because someone set us up, and I'm out here on *probation* while they use PTSD as an excuse. Y'gotta give me *something*."

I wasn't really sure what possessed me to start all that, but I'd realized halfway through how right I was. It hit me, for the first time, that Jerzy—a *good* Walker and my friend—hadn't been killed by accident. They were investigating the possibility of foul play, and *of course* there'd been foul play. The explosions, the scorch marks . . . It infuriated me. I was tired of being treated like a kid, and I was more than ready to get some damn *answers* for once.

Jay was looking at me like he was seeing someone different. He blinked and narrowed his eyes and then, to my astonishment, gave a crisp nod. "Yes, sir," he said, with more than a hint of irony. "It's not that they're what InterWorld will become, exactly; it's more that they're the section of InterWorld that deals specifically with time. We keep HEX and Binary from ruling all the worlds on the Arc, and TimeWatch keeps them from ruling the timestream. Though they've got bigger problems than Binary and HEX."

"Bigger problems? Such as—?"

Jay hesitated again, just for a second, as though he was reluctant to even speak their names. "The Techmaturges."

"The . . . ?"

"They're the things that give both Lord Dogknife and the Professor nightmares. There aren't many of them, but they're so powerful that a single glance from one could destroy a world. They've refined the arts of both magic and science so as to be nigh indestructible. And incredibly destruc*tive*. They don't want to rule all life, they want to wipe it out and start over."

"But if they can destroy worlds that easily, why haven't they won?"

"TimeWatch. I don't know exactly how they do it, but they're the ones keeping things in order."

"And they can time travel."

"You got it."

"So . . . Acacia's a—"

"Time Agent. Which means you two have a rocky road ahead of you."

I didn't really want to know, but I asked anyway. "What?"

"I know you two just met and all, but if you're anything like me—and I know you are—you're interested."

"I'm not," I tried, but Jay laughed.

"Please. I'm trying to talk to you like an adult. Act like one. You're interested, and why shouldn't you be? Sounds like she might be, too, from how she's fixated on you." My face was as red as the dirt beneath us, but I kept quiet.

"The Time Agents care about one thing, and one thing only: the future. Making sure it happens. I'd watch it around her, honestly. If she decides you might change future events, she'll take you out—and no one will question her right to do so. In judgments about time their authority is absolute. No matter what your intentions are, or how she feels about you—"

"I get it, I said." I drew a rigid index finger across my Adam's apple. *"Scchhhrreekkk."*

"You should be so lucky. She can do far worse than merely kill you. She can *erase* you. And will, if she deems it necessary for the good of continuity." Jay was as grim as I could ever recall seeing him. "To save the timestream, if she has to, she'll see that you're *expunged*."

I stared at him, logic warring with feeling—though really, the two weren't mutually exclusive. "I . . . but, how can she— What about everything I've done? If I'm *erased*, what happens to the things I've changed?"

"She fills in the gaps, fixes them herself. It wouldn't be *you* who did those things, it'd be her or someone else. She can do it," he assured me, seeing my disbelief. "And like I said, if she thinks it's best for the future that you were never in the past, she *will*."

I couldn't argue with that, but I sure as hell wanted to. After struggling for a moment and coming up blank, I pushed it aside and moved on.

"So what do I do now?"

"Go back home. Back to Base. Sit and wait."

I just stared at him. The seconds stretched on, until he chuckled.

"Didn't think you'd go for that. But you *should* go back home, at least long enough to see if they've found anything."

"What about Acacia?"

"She's a Time Agent. If it's fated for you to see her again, you will."

"But—"

It was too late; the conversation was over. I don't know if Hue shifted the focus of his lensing ability, or if Jay did it himself, but his image shimmered like oil on water and then was gone.

I felt, rather abruptly, like sitting down. So I did, half sitting and half collapsing onto the ground. I looked about, marveling once again at how everything seemed exactly the same. Even the scuffs from where I'd dragged Jay's bleeding body were still there. I winced at the thought and looked away.

Something odd struck me then, and, much as I didn't want to, I looked back at those marks. Everything was as I'd remembered it, except for one thing.

There was no blood.

I remembered, all too vividly, dragging Jay, encased in his silver suit which covered him completely, save the huge holes that had been left by the gyradon's daggerlike teeth. Blood had gushed out, violently at first, then in slower, weaker gouts, as his heart had slowed and his veins and arteries emptied. There had been enough, I remembered, to turn a large patch of the dusty ground to dark, viscous mud.

None of that remained.

The sun, I thought, *it must've*—

But there was no sun—just that swirling van Gogh sky.

I jumped to my feet. Suddenly I couldn't wait to get out

of there. Hue was hovering anxiously in front of me, pulsing colors and patterns like a supercharged kaleidoscope.

I felt something—a *presence*—behind me . . . a breeze—or a breath?—on the back of my neck. Images flashed through my head of slitted red eyes and gleaming yellow teeth. I had yet, in all my travels and missions, to come across anything as terrifying as the leader of HEX, and he still featured prominently in my dreams and moments like these, when I was sure there was *something* just behind me. . . .

Fast as I could, I Walked.

I may not have come away from that conversation completely enlightened, but I'd certainly learned enough to give me a start on things. Now, if only fate would hurry itself up and let me see Acacia again, I could learn a bit more.

I'd like to be able to say that what happened then was the call of my name in a familiar voice. I'd like to tell you that I heard it the moment I stepped into the In-Between, turned, and there she was. I'd like to tell you that, because not only would it have meant I got to see Acacia that much sooner, it would have hurt far less.

What *actually* happened was that I got shot by a laser.

I've mentioned the noise in the In-Between, so it won't come as much of a shock that I didn't hear the thing fire. It's like when you brush your hand against something really hot when you aren't looking—there's a shock of pain and a sense of *wrong*, but for an instant you're not even sure where it came from. It hurts so much that at first you can't even tell *where* it hurts.

It took a moment for my brain to sort everything out, but even before that, I'd thrown myself to the right, off the little ledge of candy-striped sand I'd been standing on. I got a single glimpse of a humanoid figure before the psychedelic chaos of the In-Between surrounded me and I whooshed, in a more-or-less controlled fall, down to a patch of grass about the size of a Volkswagen. The left side of my chest and inside upper arm were burned, and there was a hole clear through the sling covering my shoulder.

I dropped into a defensive stance, keeping an eye out above me. Whatever or whoever had shot me had to come from the same direction. Basic teleportation didn't work in the In-Between; it was too chaotic, had too many things interfering with it.

I heard it, this time—a kind of *zwipp* sound, but it was coming from behind me. And right before the sound, a nagging tug on my mind, something I recognized, a feeling as familiar as the beat of my heart . . .

Someone had just Walked nearby.

Hue had gotten behind me, and when the laser was fired again, he sort of turned into a giant, flat bit of reflective rubber. He caught the laser beam and flung it back out again, off in a different direction, snapping back into his usual sphere.

It was like watching someone stretch a balloon way out, except it didn't pop and just returned to its normal shape.

When he did, though, I could see past him. I could see the person standing there, arm still extended, laser still out. And it was not *anyone* I'd expected to see.

"What the hell are you doing?!"

"Exterminate target: Joey Harker," said J/O, and fired again.

CHAPTER ELEVEN

EVERYTHING ABOUT HIM *LOOKED* like the J/O I was used to except for the scrapes and injuries from the rockslide—and the laser pointed at me. I wasn't used to seeing it from that angle. J/O and I had gotten off to a rocky start, but we'd been teammates for two years now. I'd gotten used to the snarky comments, even given most of them back to him, but now he was *actually trying to kill me,* which was several light-years beyond snarky any way you looked at it.

Hue did his laser-bouncing trick again, but I could tell it was hurting him. He turned a pained reddish green, seeming to huddle around himself. He couldn't take much more—and here I was, on a bit of floating ground with the In-Between all around me, and no weapon.

Well, no weapon *on* me. The In-Between, however, was full of random things. . . .

I leaped off the ground patch, jumping toward what

looked like a metal trash can lid or manhole cover, except it was bright blue. I swung it around, using it as a shield just in time to deflect another laser blast as I landed on a beach ball–like sphere. It looked solid enough; unfortunately, what things look like in the In-Between isn't always what they are. The globe popped like a soap bubble (*bub-bell*, whispered the memory of my little brother's voice), and I fell about ten feet onto a path that smelled like too-sweet perfume and looked like the road to Oz.

J/O landed in front of me a moment later, and I used my makeshift shield to deflect another blast. A single look at him told me that trying to reason with him would be useless—he was in serious Terminator mode. His gaze locked on me as it would on a target, nothing more, and I knew he'd just keep coming.

"J/O, in accordance with InterWorld's laws and code of conduct, I order you to cease fire!" Knowing it was futile didn't really help. He was still my friend and teammate; what else could I do?

He ignored the command, as I'd assumed he would, and fired again. The shot was aimed for my head, and I brought the lid shield up again. There was a flare of red light all around it, and I could see tiny, veinlike cracks spreading across the surface. I was going to have to find a new shield.

I hurled the thing à la Captain America, silently thanking my Alternative Phys Ed teacher for training us in the dubiously useful art of discus throwing. J/O brought his arm up to block it, and I heard a crack as it made contact with his retractable laser. Hoping fervently that my improvised weapon had broken his built-in one, I jumped off the path and opened my senses for another portal. I could Walk around in the In-Between, so long as I was careful; doing it too much could get very disorienting, and if there was anywhere in the Altiverse you *didn't* want to get lost, it was here. Well, here and the Nowhere-at-All.

There wasn't a portal near enough for me to Walk through, so I couldn't get back to Base, but I spotted some shafts of light filtering through a floating porthole. I snatched one of them out of the air, or what passed for air here. It was warm, and too bright to look at directly. I wasn't sure if it was sharp, but I was hoping it would serve to distract him enough that I could . . . I wasn't sure, exactly. I didn't really want to hurt him.

He, on the other hand, obviously had no problem with hurting me. . . .

There was a shimmer behind me and I turned, twirling the light beam around in a figure eight. His next laser blast (no such luck of its being broken, apparently) ricocheted off my makeshift sword and I felt, for a moment, like a Jedi. J/O had turned to the dark side and I was forced to fight him, whether I liked it or not.

"J/O," I tried again, but I didn't have time to do much

else. His laser retracted and he strode forward, grabbing one of the light beams for himself. Something clicked in the back of my mind—he wasn't just trying to kill me, he was trying to *beat* me. His laser was a better weapon than the light sword, but he wasn't relying on the laser. He was accepting a challenge, taking an opportunity to beat me in an even fight. That meant he was motivated, at least in part, by his ego.

And that meant that, regardless of why he was fighting me, the J/O I'd known was still in there.

Unfortunately, I wasn't going to get the chance to try reaching him. I'd seen J/O sword fight once before, in a duel to the death on the *Malefic*. He'd won, and it hadn't been a close call. J/O was *good*, and the likelihood of my getting sliced into sushi was growing with every parry and riposte.

I sprang backward, swiping my sword through a floating blob of jellylike substance, sending bits and pieces of it splattering toward my former teammate. I let go of the light-beam sword at the same time, not waiting around to find out if I'd hit anything. My shoulder *hurt*, as did the areas that had been burned by his first laser blast, and I had to find a portal and Walk back to InterWorld. I had to tell them something was wrong with J/O.

There was an explosion behind me, and I didn't even stop to see what it was. A blast of heat ruffled my hair as I jumped again. I had no idea where I was going, but with my shoulder as messed up as it was, climbing wasn't really an option. The only place I could go was down. I wondered if the In-Between had a "ground" or anything like it.

I kept running, sometimes hurling things behind me, sometimes catching a glimpse of him right at my heels if I jumped or ran or fell past a reflective surface. I was just barely able to stay ahead of him, and I wasn't going to be able to keep it up. He had the advantage of being a cyborg, never mind his *not* having a fractured shoulder and several bruised ribs. Which were all starting to ache abominably.

I'm not entirely sure what happened next. One instant, I was running through an upside-down forest with odd-looking giant flowers instead of trees, and the next I was sprawled flat on my back in a great amount of pain. I was too disoriented to even see what I'd run into, but in the In-Between it could have been anything. Instinct propelled me to my feet and I cast about for a portal, but no luck. J/O was closing in, and I had nowhere to go.

"J/O," I tried again, one hand clutching my shoulder. "I don't know what's gotten into you, but quit it! Do a hard restart or something! Reprogram!"

"Target confirmed," he said in our voice, which I'd long ago gotten used to but was still so odd sometimes, especially when it was saying something like this. "Joey Harker." He raised his arm, laser engaging again, aimed—

"Call me Joe," I said. As last words went, they were maybe not the best I could have come up with, but they seemed appropriate. A red light flared at the mouth of J/O's built-in weapon, and I looked around in a last-ditch effort to find something I could use.

There was the sound of a laser firing, and I felt nothing. Literally, though it took me a moment to realize I hadn't been hit.

"Unexpected variable," said J/O, just as I saw the figure hovering about three yards from us. "Acacia Jones."

"Acacia!" Her hair whipped around her face as she turned toward me, arm still extended and holding something that looked like it was more likely to unlock a car door than save my life, even though that's exactly what it had just done. My relief at seeing her was quickly replaced by worry; she'd just made herself a target, and J/O was taking aim again.

She launched herself—I wasn't sure how, but it seemed to have something to do with her shoes—across the In-Between in my direction, using the car-beeper thing to shoot at J/O. I was reminded of when Hue had saved my life from the agents of HEX by hurtling toward me at full speed and teleporting us both out. Acacia did much the same thing, colliding with me as a burst of purple light enveloped us. We fell through nothing, and pain exploded once again in my shoulder as I landed on my back. I gasped—and opened my eyes to Acacia, backlit by a brilliant blue sky.

She was half on top of me, the ends of her dark hair

brushing against my cheeks and lips. I blinked as a few strands got in my eyes, and felt her get to her feet. By the time I'd rubbed my eyes to clear my vision, she was standing, looking off into the distance.

I sat up carefully, using one arm to push myself to my feet. The grass beneath me was green, the sky above me blue, and puffy white clouds made their way across it. The sun was just climbing higher in the sky; I guessed the time to be around eleven A.M. or so, assuming this world counted time similarly to my old one. The air was clean and crisp, a little cool, tinged with a slightly acrid smell.

"Close call," Acacia said suddenly, turning to look amiably at me. "Hey, Joe. It's been a while."

Ordinarily, I would have waved that off and asked where we were, or how she'd known to find me. I would have just been glad to see her again, and forgotten all about Jay's warning.

But now I knew she was a Time Agent, and that meant I had different questions.

"How long is 'a while'?"

She paused, giving me a considering look. "Since the last time I had to jet. When we punched it."

"I remember. How long ago was that for you?"

She turned fully toward me and put her hands on her hips. "I'm guessing you know, then."

"Yeah."

"That I'm a Time Agent."

"Yep."

"Okay. Good question. Would you believe me if I said it's been a few years?"

I paused, considering that. I looked her over carefully, checking what I saw with what I remembered; she didn't seem any older. She was wearing mostly the same clothing she'd worn before; her hair was the same length. She sounded the same.

"No," I said finally, trying to sound certain. I was rewarded with a bright, mischievous grin.

"Good answer! It's been, what, three days for you?" I shrugged; honestly, with the rockslide and Jerzy's death, I wasn't even sure how many days ago I'd seen her. It felt like both yesterday and forever.

"It's been about a week for me. Your ship, ah, *punching it* was a little disorienting. It messed with me something major, actually. I was sick for two days, couldn't eat a thing." She stretched her arms over her head and clasped them behind her neck casually, turning this way and that to look over our new surroundings.

"Why?"

"Because you were flickering through multiple dimensions at warp speed. I'm a Time Agent, Joe. My grip on this plane is a little more tenuous than yours. I have to temporarily anchor anywhere I go."

That made a certain amount of sense. "So we messed with your anchor."

"More like I lost it completely. Have you ever been really, really seasick?"

I shook my head. "I went over a waterfall in a barrel once."

She laughed. "Well, it was probably kind of like that." She paused, tilting her head. "You hear that?"

I listened. Off in the distance, there was scattered percussion, faint pops and booms. "Yeah. What is it?"

"C'mon." She took my hand.

"I remember learning about this in high school." We were standing on a ridge just inside a copse of trees, watching the figures in their life-or-death chess match below. "The Battle of the Somme, 1916. Third period history, with Mr. Luru."

"So do I," Acacia said, though she grinned when I looked at her. "I remember learning it," she clarified. "Not in your third period history class. I was here, though. Field trip. We watched from right over there." She pointed.

"Is what they say in all the science fiction novels true? That you create a paradox by being in the same place at the same time, and it could destroy the world, or make more of you?"

"Nope. It's not possible. When you enter a timestream, you anchor to it and stay anchored—once you're there, you're part of it. If you drop anchor, you can slip out of the timestream and come back, but you won't run into yourself because you're not there, you're here."

I tried to follow that, I really did. And I didn't want to admit that she'd lost me, but . . . "So . . . you can actually affect anything, as many times as you want?"

"Not exactly. Since I'm anchored here, if I go fifty years into the future and stay there for a week, I can only come back a week from today. If I drop anchor and go somewhere else, and anchor in a different timestream, I can come back to this exact same day and not run into myself, but anything I affected while I was here is still affected. *That's* where we have to be careful about paradox."

"So why can't you just do the same thing over and over?"

"For one, because it makes us really, really timesick." She noticed my blank look and clarified. "Imagine every time in your life when you've been really sick to your stomach—every carnival ride, every storm at sea, every touch of flu, or—"

"Got the concept. Thanks."

"Then imagine all those times overlaid, one on top of the other, so that you feel them both separately and all at—"

"Which part of 'got the concept' is giving you trouble?"

She grinned again.

You know those memories you have that seem frozen in time, like a snapshot? Even if you don't have a picture to look at, you remember every detail. Oftentimes right after the moment's passed, you know it'll be one of those memories—everything seems to slow down, and that one picture stays stuck in your mind.

The second I felt someone Walk, the very instant I heard the *vwip* of the laser, I knew that second would be with me forever, the moment right before her smile turned into a gasp.

I turned, calculating the trajectory of the assault: It had come from behind me, slightly to the left. I dove forward, trying to get in close so J/O wouldn't have time to use his laser again. He brought up an arm to block my first strike, and my second, but my third got through. I had to keep him on the defensive. I had to get him away from Acacia.

I couldn't see her well, but the glimpses I caught when I was ducking or kicking told me she was still alive. More than that, she was doing something—her green circuitry nails were glowing and sparking, both of her hands pressed over where I was assuming her wound was, somewhere on her stomach. I wondered if she could regenerate. I hoped so.

"Target locked: Joey Harker," said J/O, which was really more insult to injury as he said it just after catching me with an admittedly nice right hook. My back hit the ground again and I felt my ribs protest; I wasn't going to be able to take much more of this, and I was getting a little tired of that being the case.

"How the hell did you follow us?" Acacia's voice was remarkably steady for someone who had just been shot.

J/O glanced past me, to where Acacia was getting to her

feet. He offered no answer, merely extending his laser arm once again.

"You can't Walk through time," she persisted, tracing the outline of a badge in the air. It glowed green for a moment, flashing an official-looking seal with her name on it before vanishing. "As an official Agent of the TimeWatch Organization, I order you to declare yourself." I cast her an incredulous look as she limped over to stand beside me, the badge moving in front of her. Did she really think that was going to work? (Never mind that I'd tried the exact same thing, in my own way. . . .)

J/O laughed. "We do not answer to your TimeWatch."

"If you've stolen our technology, believe me, you *will*."

"We do not need your technology, Time Agent. We know your very *essence*, and we will follow it anywhere."

Acacia straightened up abruptly, putting a hand on my shoulder. Her circuit-board nails flashed, and I felt something a little like a static shock. "We'll see."

J/O vanished. At least, that's what I thought had happened, in the first instant—then he was back, but the trees around him were different. The sun and moon were flickering like a strobe light; the ground beneath us was grass, sand, water, grass again. I clung to Acacia's hand, watching the world around us change, watching J/O flicker in and out, sometimes solidly there, sometimes see-through, sometimes only a shadow or an impression, just for a second.

It was a little like punching it, except we weren't moving. We were standing absolutely still, and the world was changing around us. The trees grew taller, then shorter, one was struck by lightning, then was whole and green again. I couldn't tell if we were going forward or backward; then I realized it was both. A figure walked past me and then split into two; one went left, the other right. More and more figures began to form around us; soldiers, mostly, running and jumping or ducking and hiding, often splitting into two different versions, one of them falling and lying still, the other crawling to safety—and all the while J/O, flickering in and out, came ever closer.

I could sympathize with how Acacia had felt on Base Town, when we'd gone into overdrive. I would rather have sailed over the waterfall in a barrel again, even with all the stitches I'd needed.

Finally, *finally* it stopped. I didn't even know where we were now, but I knew there was a bush nearby, and I knew I had to rid myself of anything I'd eaten in the last few hours. I would have been humiliated, except I could hear Acacia doing the same thing a few feet away.

I recovered more quickly, and was able to crawl over and rub her back while she curled there miserably, gasping for breath. "Are you okay?" I managed, and she nodded. "Here." I pulled a little flask from my boot, uncorking it and offering it to her. She looked at me like I was absolutely nuts. "Trust me." I took her hand and pressed the flask into it, again enjoying knowing something she didn't. I remembered the first time Jay'd offered it to me, and I'd assumed it was alcohol; I guessed Acacia was doing the same thing.

She smelled it hesitantly, then took a sip; I couldn't help a smile as her brows lifted in surprise, and her features relaxed. "It's pretty good, huh?" She took another sip and handed it back to me, shifting around to use my knee as a pillow. She nodded, and I took a sip from the flask myself. I've never gotten a straight answer about what it was, and I frankly didn't care—all I knew was that it wasn't alcohol and therefore didn't have any of the nasty side effects, and no matter how small a sip you took, you immediately felt like you were rising from the softest bed in the nicest weather, with the smell of your favorite breakfast in the air. You felt like you were ready to take on the world.

I finally took a moment to look around, not that I could see much. Everything was gray and foggy, covered in a thick mist. Shadows and shapes moved through it; and while it wasn't the kind of mist that obscured my vision, it just made everything a little hazy. It was like looking at something through a patterned glass window: You could see shapes, but not make out details.

"Where are we?"

"That's hard to answer." Acacia's voice drifted up from my lap, weak and strained.

"Is there a better question?"

I think she smiled, but I couldn't quite tell. "You could ask where we aren't."

"Okay. Where aren't we?"

"Anywhere." She took a deep breath, shifting to sit up. I helped her, keeping a hand on her shoulder to steady her. "We're not anywhere."

She looked awful. She still seemed dizzy and had the shakes, and her skin was pale and clammy. I offered her the flask again, but she shook her head.

"We're not anywhere? So we're nowhere? I've been in the Nowhere-at-All, and this isn't—"

"No, it's not the same." She took another breath, raking her hair back behind her ears. One of her nails was broken, split to the quick and bleeding. "I dropped anchor. Without a destination."

It was starting to make a little more sense, sort of. "So we fell through the world?"

She shook her head. "We fell through *time*."

I looked around at the figures, misty and distorted, walking around us. It was like they were overlaid—one would walk right past, then bend down to pick something up from the ground. Then it would straighten and go on its way, except there would still be a figure standing there, looking at whatever it was. Then that one would go off in a different direction. They were all over the place, sometimes even walking right through me.

"Are you okay? He shot you."

She nodded, moving part of her shirt aside to show me. The shirt itself was seared through, but the skin beneath it was unburned. Red, yes, with the faint start of bruising, but unburned. "Skin shield."

"Is that . . . like a suit, or something?"

"Sort of. It's not really something you put on like clothing—it's just a . . . an energy shield. I've gotta recharge it, now . . . that was a strong blast." She sighed, running her fingers over the area. Her fingernails sparked, circuitry pulsing with green light, and a thought struck me.

"Can you recharge this?" I held out the little shield disk I still had, the one I'd found on the mountain. Acacia took it from me, turning it over thoughtfully.

"I think so. It's the same kind of thing as my skin shield, just . . . well, less advanced. No offense."

I shrugged. Acacia held her hand out, palm up, fingers bent and apart. She rested the disk on her fingernails. A spark of electricity jumped from one to the next, around to four of her fingers; one of her nails was still broken. The disk glowed faintly blue.

"Neat trick," I commented. She smiled, but didn't respond.

I counted the seconds until she was done. Twenty, not the full thirty it usually took to fully charge a disk. Acacia's fingernails were more powerful than anything we had.

She handed it back, and I powered it up. The surface of it flashed, then displayed a blue serial number: FB242.

"That can't be right," I muttered. Acacia looked at me questioningly.

"Did it work?"

"Yeah, but . . . this is the one I lost. The one the quartermaster got mad at me for. The one I had to leave on Earth FΔ98^6."

"Where did you find it?"

"At the . . ." I realized I hadn't told her about the rockslide yet. Maybe she already knew. "On the mountain. On top."

"Are you sure it's the same one?"

"Yes." She looked skeptical. "I'm absolutely sure. The number is FB two forty-two, and my mother's birthday is February twenty-fourth. I remember noticing that when I checked it out. It's the same one."

"So how'd it get there?"

"I don't *know*. I saw it fall. I left it behind; I didn't have a choice." I powered it down, clipping it back to my belt. This was all getting immensely confusing. "I was trying to throw it to Jo when she was falling, but Joaquim grabbed her and they both Walked. . . ."

"Could someone have gone back to get it?"

"I don't . . ." I sighed, running a hand through my hair and looking up at the sky. It was both sunny and cloudy, and dark storm clouds loomed off to the west. If I looked closely,

I could see rain falling around us, but we weren't wet. The ghostly figures still milled about, walking or jogging or falling, everywhere I looked.

And one of them looked familiar.

"He found us!" I started to scramble to my feet, but Acacia grabbed my wrist.

"No," she tugged on my arm, and I paused. "He hasn't. He's looking, but he can't see us. If he could, he'd be *here*. He'd be clear."

"*Can* he find us?" I sat back down.

She shook her head, then brought up a hand to rub her temple in frustration. "I don't know. He shouldn't be able to. He shouldn't have been able to Walk through time. Walkers can't *do* that, right?" She looked at me.

"No," I said, "except for relativistic and sidereal changes from world to world." Think of going from New York to LA—that's TimeWalking in a way. But you expend a certain amount of time traveling between them, whether it's just a few hours by a Boeing 747 or a few months by a Conestoga. "The closest we come is the In-Between, but that's to get us from one world to another; it's all about *where* we go, not *when*." I had a sudden, dizzying flash of the awesome math it required just to move about outside time: to go six months forward or back instantaneously and not wind up floating, flash frozen, in space because the Earth had moved out from under you on its merry way around the sun. Sir Isaac had had things simpler when time was serenely separate from the rest of the universe and not all bound up as part of space.

"*I* don't know how to, anyway," I told her. "No one I know knows how, unless they've been hiding it from me. We didn't learn it on InterWorld."

She scooted around so that her back was to mine and we were leaning against each other for support. I leaned back with some relief; my ribs were killing me. "What did he say?" she asked. "He said he didn't answer to TimeWatch. What else?"

I thought—as much as was possible, anyway, with pain still clamoring at my nerve endings. "Uh . . . he said he didn't need your technology. And that he was . . . anchored . . . ? No. *Fixed* on our souls."

"Essence," Acacia said assuredly. "He said 'essence.' That he was fixed on your essence, and he'd follow it anywhere. But that's not how we do it. It's not TimeWatch technology. We can track people, but not like . . ." I felt her sit up a little straighter against me, felt her breathing quicken.

"Acacia?"

"They do that," she said, her voice shaky. "*They* do that."

"'They'?"

"The things we're sworn to fight. But he wasn't—"

"A Techmaturge?"

She whirled around, and I almost fell at the abrupt lack of support. "How do you know about them?" Her stare was intense. I heard the ghostly echo of Jay's voice: *erase you . . . she'll see that you're expunged . . .*

"How'd I know you were a Time Agent? Simple. I did my own research." It was mostly true, and I wasn't sure how to explain that I'd been told by the psychic imprint of my former mentor. I mean, she'd probably believe me, but it seemed better not to tell her.

After a moment she took a breath, looking up toward the foggy gray-blue sky. "Okay. He can't *actually* have Techmaturge power, or we'd be dead. But he still managed to fix on our essence and follow. *How*?"

"Well, what else did he say?" We were both silent for a moment, thinking.

Finally, Acacia shook her head. "He just said he didn't need our technology, and that he'd fixed on our essence."

Something pinged in the back of my mind. "No, hold on. He said 'we.' He said, 'W*e* don't need your technology.'"

"'We'?" Acacia looked at me.

"J/O doesn't talk like that. He says *I*, first person. He may be a cyborg, but he's always been his own cyborg. The only robots I know of who refer to themselves in the collective are the—"

It hit me all at once, and I thought I was going to be sick again. "The Binary," I managed, as Acacia just looked at me.

"You said he's a cyborg."

"He comes from a world closer to the technological end of

the Arc. More advanced in science. They inject you with programming microchips the day you're born. People live longer, are healthier, all of that."

"Could he have been a traitor this whole time?"

"No," I said, a little too forcefully. She raised an eyebrow; I took a breath. "No, I don't think so. He's been on my team for so many missions; he was captured by HEX once—he's just like me. He's *one* of me. I think . . ." I fell silent, and Acacia nudged me with a shoulder.

"You think what?"

"I think this happened recently. Like when we got Joaquim. We were on a Binary world, and J/O had to hack into the mainframe to get some information for the Old Man. Something backfired, and . . . he was unconscious when I rejoined the team. He was out for a few days."

"They infected him," murmured Acacia, confirming what I'd just realized myself.

"Doesn't he have antispyware or something?" I wondered aloud. "Even my world has that, and we're not half as advanced!"

Acacia snorted, but I was too upset to find it even faintly funny. My friend was a member of the Binary now. No wonder he'd been trying to kill me. I put my head in my hands.

"Hey, it's okay, Joe. We can fix him." She paused, then went on, though seemingly reluctant to do so. "I . . . this doesn't solve how he followed us, though. The Binary can't time travel, either. The only ones I know who can are the Techmaturges, but even their ability is limited. That's how we stay on top."

"If they can time travel, couldn't one of them have come back and given him the power?"

"They can't transfer it like that. It's much more complicated than that. Every time someone tries to change the time line, alternate worlds are created. And I'd know if one was here, or had been here."

"How?"

"Because it's my job to know. We keep *close* track of these guys. There aren't many, but—"

"But their power can destroy worlds with a single glance, I know." I ran my hands through my hair, grabbing two fistfuls of it in frustration. "I have to get back. I don't know if he's just after me, or everything—but InterWorld might be in danger."

I felt her sigh, felt her hair brush against the back of my neck as she looked away. "I don't think you should go back yet, Joe."

"Why not?"

"Because it's not safe."

My response was a laugh that came out a whole lot more bitter than I intended it to. "*Nowhere's* safe right now, Acacia. My team and most of another just barely made it back alive from a simple capture-the-flag mission. One of us *didn't*.

And we were just followed through time by a Walker, some-one who's supposed to be on *my team*—" I stopped, but not because Acacia was talking. I wasn't even sure what she was saying—telling me to calm down, maybe, or explaining why she thought it wasn't safe. I wasn't listening. I was thinking about the rockslide and J/O's virus and the shield disk. I was thinking about how he'd been on standby for a while, and I hadn't seen him until we went on our training mission. I was thinking about how he'd still been unconscious in the infir-mary when I'd signed out to go off Base.

Someone had to have gone back to FΔ98^6 to get the shield disk—but it hadn't been him. He'd been plugged in right up until the capture-the-flag game, and the Base Town sensors automatically filed it if someone Walked off world. I'd seen the sign-outs before I left; J/O hadn't left Base.

He'd been plugged in, though. To the infirmary. Could he have gotten access to the sheets, scrambled it so that his name wasn't there? No, he couldn't have done both, not in that amount of time. . . .

The more I thought about it, the more certain I was: Someone else had gone back to Earth FΔ98^6. Someone else had picked up the lost disk, recharged it, and brought it on a simple training mission instead of turning it in. Someone who'd been in the rockslide and survived.

"There's someone else." I cut Acacia off midsentence, gaze locked on the silhouette of J/O as he Walked, trying to find us. "There's another traitor in InterWorld. He's there *right now*. I have to—"

I never saw her move. All I knew was that I felt an abrupt prick at the base of my neck, like something had stung or bitten me, and then my entire body grew uncomfortably warm. I couldn't move. The shapes around me were growing fuzzier, my vision was suddenly filled with a faint purple glow, and static crackled in my ears.

I didn't even feel myself falling, but I definitely knew it when I hit the ground. Still, the pain seemed far away, held just outside my body by that shining purple light. I tried to get up, or at least roll over and look at Acacia, but my limbs weren't responding to my brain. For one brief, horrified moment, I remembered when Lady Indigo of HEX had laid a spell on me. There had been a little voice of reason inside me, screaming at me to run, but I'd simply stayed at her side and obeyed her every command. For an instant, I was terrified that Acacia had done the same. Then she stepped into my line of vision, knelt, and put a hand to my head. She looked sad.

The ground beneath us vanished, and once again we fell through time.

The TimeWatch headquarters—what little I could see of it—seemed a lot like InterWorld. It wasn't that Acacia had put a spell on me, exactly, but she'd somehow disabled my motor functions. I was only half conscious when I felt ground beneath me again. It was white tile, shining with the reflection of the bright lights above us. Voices rang out around me, one of them Acacia's, but I couldn't make out the words.

She had me in some kind of antigravity grip. I occasionally saw sparks of purple and green around me, saw her nails glowing as she took me through the corridors. I couldn't tell if I was walking or not, or if my feet were even touching the ground. Everything was bright and clean and shining, the colors all soft and muted, beautifully luminescent. After only a few rooms we stopped, and I was moved to some kind of gurney. Now I could see everything above me, and I forgot about worrying where I was going or what was happening as I gazed up into the domed sky.

I couldn't tell if it was an open roof or a window or if it was painted on—but it was beautiful. It looked like the night sky except white instead of dark blue, with a thousand sunsets swirling behind the misty clouds. The "stars" were all blues and greens and peaches, lavenders and rosy hues; and there was no single sun or moon but rather thousands of them, small and large and all sharing the sky. Some parts grew darker, others lighter, then they'd switch, giving the impression of a pulse or faint heartbeat. It wasn't just in that one room, either. It was everywhere we went, down hallways and through corridors, with Acacia pushing me along like a patient on the way to surgery.

That was an unsettling comparison.

Gradually, I became aware of hushed voices around me. I tried to turn my head to either side, and couldn't. I could just barely see figures out of the corner of my vision, hazy and indistinct, like those we'd just left at the time vortex. They were whispering. The static in my ears had died down a little, and I could make out someone saying "Is that him?"

Acacia took me through several halls and rooms, and into something resembling an elevator. I couldn't tell if we were going up or down, but I assumed down because when we got out, the sky was gone. It wasn't as bright anymore. The walls were gray instead of white.

And there were bars.

Acacia moved me through one set of bars, into a small room. I became aware of the air on my skin again; it was a neutral temperature, not hot or cold. I could turn my head and flex my fingers. I saw Acacia as she walked back through the bars the same way we'd entered, like a ghost. I saw the green light on her fingernails fade as she gripped the bars—which seemed quite solid—for a moment. "I'm sorry, Joe," she said, and walked away.

I could move again. And I was a prisoner of TimeWatch.

CHAPTER TWELVE

"SHE'S TRYING TO HELP you."

My guard was a man who didn't look like me at all, which had taken some getting used to. Actually, he looked like a normal guy, the kind I might've seen walking down the street in my world, the kind who may have been a policeman or a businessman. He stood up tall, and hadn't looked at me even once since he'd planted himself as an immovable object in front of my cell.

I didn't say "door" because there wasn't one, from what I could tell. The bars were simple, went from the floor to the ceiling, and I didn't see anything resembling hinges anywhere. When I'd first entered, the cell had seemed quite complex; I'd felt my passage through it like a moment of cold fog, and when Acacia had left me I'd seen the bars ripple for an instant, like disturbed water.

I'd been stuck here for hours, unable to do anything but

pace, and my guard had—until now—not lent himself very well to conversation.

"Why do you say that?" At his silence, I felt my temper—which was precarious to begin with—slip a notch. "Oh, come on. You've been doing that statue routine for hours; now that you've started talking, you don't get to just stop again. Why do you think she's trying to help me?"

"She said so."

I gestured at my surroundings. "How is *this* helping, exactly?"

"You're safe here."

"I didn't *ask* to be kept safe!"

"It's her job."

I couldn't help thinking of what Jay had told me through Hue, and I took a deep breath before asking. "Which is, exactly?"

"To protect you."

"It's her job to protect the future," I snapped. "Where does that include electrocuting me and shoving me in a cell?"

He turned to face me at that, meeting my gaze for the first time since he'd come down here. "You *are* the future, Joseph Harker."

Something in my stomach knotted into a hard ball, and my tongue suddenly felt too big for my mouth. I was just one in an army—an army of me, yes, but that was just the point. They were *all* me. He had to mean all of us. He had to mean InterWorld, right?

I have no idea what I would have said to that, if I'd gotten the chance to respond. Right at that moment, however, a large man in a black suit came up behind the guard, clapping a hand on his shoulder. The guard jumped—for a moment I thought, from his expression, that he was under attack. He took a single step back, turning and bowing his head, then left without another word to me.

The man in the suit was tall and well muscled, wearing black sunglasses with reflective lenses and some kind of earpiece. Honestly, he looked so much like a stereotypical bodyguard that I expected to see someone else with him, maybe a small, important-looking man or a woman in a jeweled tiara. He was alone, though, and I could tell he was looking at me as he made a gesture, and a door-sized portion of the bars simply evaporated.

"You are to come with me, Joseph Harker." His mouth hadn't moved, but I knew the words had come from him. How, I wasn't sure, but I'd seen far stranger things in my time at InterWorld.

"Where's Acacia?"

"You will not find her here if you attempt to run. Do not bother."

I nodded my acquiescence. As he raised his hand to make another gesture toward the bars, I ducked around him, darting through. I put my hand to the shield disk at my belt, activating it in case he attempted to stop me with a blaster or something even as I wondered why Acacia had let me keep it—and then I was on my back, staring up at him. He'd just suddenly been *there*, in front of me, with no indication of how he'd gotten there. Almost like he'd Walked, though I hadn't sensed a portal . . .

"Do not bother attempting to run," he said again, in the exact same tone he'd used before. He sounded bored.

He reached toward me. I rolled sideways, only to feel his fingers close about the back of my tunic—and he *lifted me*, as though I weighed nothing. I wasn't even surrounded by the green light this time; it wasn't a gravity repulsor field, or whatever Acacia had used. I kicked at him, not sure what I was expecting this time. I figured he'd have some fancy trick to counter it, but why not give it a shot anyway?

My foot struck what should have been a nerve bundle on his thigh, but he simply . . . didn't react. At all. I felt flesh beneath his clothing, but there was not a flinch, not a wince, not an exhalation of breath in response to my attack. Finally, figuring I should do the smart thing and give up for real this time, I spread my hands in surrender.

He set me down but did not release my shirt. I didn't much care; I wasn't really interested in attempting to run again. Not if I were likely to run into more like him, which I imagined I was. Best to gather information about where I was first.

"Where am I going?" At his silence, I persisted. "You said I was to come with you. Where are we going?"

"InterWorld Base Town." His tone still had no emotion at all.

"Oh. You could have told me that when you let me out of the cell. I wouldn't have run." He remained silent yet again, so I committed myself to learning my surroundings as we walked through the halls.

As before, the hallways were gray and colorless, floor-to-ceiling bars lining them at intervals. At first, all the cells looked empty; then I noticed odd shadows within them, some of them humanoid and others not, some moving and some sitting (or otherwise being still; some of them were so shapeless it was impossible to tell). I listened, but heard nothing. It was more than a little unnerving.

We walked through several hallways like that, my escort immediately behind me with his hand gripping my shirt, until we were once again beneath the pastel "sky." There was no elevator this time. We simply walked through halls until we came to a larger room, better lit with that sky crawling across the ceiling. As far as I could tell, we'd walked in a straight line, yet somehow arrived in one of the upper floors. Unless the roof-window-sky-whatever was on the lower floors, too. I wasn't sure.

The room was empty, and I took this opportunity to look around as we walked. I'd only been able to look in one direction the last time I was here, if it was even the same area. The walls looked almost like those of a nice hotel lobby; the room was circular, the walls a rosy beige color. Artwork hung on them, abstractly pretty scenes of ships at sea, lighthouses, birds in flight. I looked down, tracing the gold lines etched into the floor until I recognized the pattern as a nautical star. The theme seemed to make perfect sense, somehow—just as something else didn't.

"Why send me back home, if Acacia told me it isn't safe?"

"The council decided."

"Are you on the council?"

"No."

"Who is?"

"Councilors."

His tone was *still* completely emotionless, the words somehow delivered from that impassive face, but I was pretty well certain he was being snide.

"So who are you?"

"Your guide. Watch your step."

I glanced down; there was, in fact, a step into the next room, if it even was a room. The floor was completely black, to the point where I doubted my foot would come into contact with anything. It did, though, and it seemed somehow firmer than the marble I'd been standing on previously.

"Good luck, Joseph Harker." His hand released my shirt, and I turned to look at him—and encountered only blackness. I put a hand out, and it brushed against a firm wall that had the texture of static. The room was completely black, yet I could see my hand and arm as clearly as if it was broad daylight. I saw all the way to my shoes when I looked down, though nothing but sheer blackness surrounded me.

Sample acquired.

I wasn't sure anyone had spoken, yet somehow the words hung in the silence.

Timestream found. Path mapping.

A small light appeared in my peripheral vision, then another, and another, until I was surrounded by a field of stars. Stars I recognized. Constellations I hadn't seen in I didn't even know how long. The Little and Big Dippers, Orion, Cassiopeia, the Lion. The North Star.

I didn't realize I was smiling until they shifted, whirling and swirling around me until it was a constant stream of light, and then—and the feeling was familiar enough now that I recognized it—I fell through time.

The landing wasn't as easy as before.

I mean, it hadn't really been *easy*, what with the vomiting the first time and the dizziness and being held captive the second. Thing is, I'd stayed conscious for all that.

I don't know how long I was out, or even *why* I was out in the first place. I just knew that my bed consisted of rocks, pebbles, and shards of glass, and I tasted blood in my mouth as I came to. My head ached like someone had it in a vise, and my vision was so blurry I could hardly see anything.

I slowly pushed myself to my hands and knees, then my feet. The smell of smoke hung in the air, and wherever I was was silent as the grave.

This wasn't right. My guard hadn't spoken all that much, but I did remember him saying I was going back to Inter-World. Was I not there yet? Did I have to Walk somewhere else first?

My vision was clearing, allowing me little details here and there. The sun was bright above me, which was not only unhelpful to both my headache and the watering of my eyes, it was outright betraying my mental image of the place when I'd smelled the smoke. I'd assumed it would be overcast, dark. There was no smoke anywhere, nor fire, but I felt ash covering my hands as I rubbed them together. I was in what must have once been a garden, a path of pebbles and sand (and ash and glass . . .) moving precisely through the twisted, blackened remains of bushes and trees.

Gravel crunched beneath my feet as I walked, slowly, taking everything in. Peering between the scorched limbs lining the path afforded me glimpses of long, rectangular boxes, sitting silently in the gardens. Long, silver boxes. The kind Jay had been sent away in, and Jerzy.

I started to run.

There was a structure up ahead, an entrance, just where I

knew it would be. Where I'd walked in alongside Jo after Jerzy's funeral, berating myself for not having taken her hand.

The door didn't slide open as I approached—there wasn't one, just a twisted scrap of metal half blocking the entryway. I climbed over it, waiting for that maddeningly calm voice to recognize and greet me. I was met with silence.

The halls didn't look familiar, yet I knew exactly where to go. Some of the doors were still sealed, but it took no strength at all to pry them open. The computer was off-line, the mechanisms just ordinary gears and wheels with nothing to lock them down. No power. There was no power in the entire base—I could see only by the light filtering in shafts from the holes in the walls and roof, motes of ash and dust stirring frantically as I passed. When the sun went down, I'd be left in darkness.

I found a blaster halfway down a hall, and took it; I was immensely grateful for the feel of it in my hand, until it fell apart. Literally. It broke in two. The metal at the grip was rusted almost through. I stood there for a few moments in the hallway, the noise seeming impossibly loud in the silence, but nothing stirred. Nothing at all.

I ran faster, bolting through the hallways and leaping over debris, through doors and around corners. Even though everything looked different, things were still naggingly similar; I knew where everything was. I found the Old Man's office with not a single wrong turn.

The scorch marks were the worst, here. The furniture was overturned, obviously having been used as a barricade at some point. The huge silver desk Josetta always sat behind was on its side, laser burns marring the smooth finish. The plush chairs and patterned oval rug were nothing but ash and dust. The door to the Old Man's office was caved in, rusted and splattered with a dried, flaky substance I didn't want to inspect more closely.

Everyone was gone.

InterWorld was destroyed.

CHAPTER THIRTEEN

I WAS REMINDED OF the time I'd sat upon the surface of an unknown planet, Jay's body at my side, and wept. I'd cried for the loss of someone I'd just met, someone who'd nevertheless saved my life a dozen times by then. I'd cried for myself, for the loneliness of knowing I was changed forever. For the family I doubted I'd ever see again. For how everything was different. I'd cried until a shadow passed over me, and InterWorld came to pick me up and take Jay home.

This time, I cried for the loss of my home, the second one I'd had to say good-bye to. For the loss of my second family, even the ones I hadn't known as well. For the fact that I'd been too late.

For how Acacia had betrayed me.

After a while I stood, brushing the ash off my hands so I could wipe the tears from my face. I climbed over the door, into the Old Man's office. It was ransacked: his desk overturned, papers scattered everywhere. I gave a thought to going through them, then decided I didn't care. It was too dim in here to read, probably even too dim to find what I wanted, but I looked anyway. I looked for the picture I'd seen before, of him and Acacia. I wanted it to tell me why I'd trusted her, why *he'd* trusted her.

The picture didn't tell me anything—I never found it. Instead, when I put a hand on the Old Man's desk, it flashed a bright blue, so bright I had to look away. A jolt of adrenaline went through me; it was the first thing that had reacted to my presence since I arrived. I was on my feet and back against the wall in a second, racking my mind for any memory of the Old Man's security systems.

The light was condensing, forming into sections, then squiggles, then letters, then words.

Joey Harker, they said. *Do not panic.*

The Old Man's desk was talking to me.

Traced your signal, it said. *Same world, same plane—in the future. Thousands of years.*

I felt my knees go weak with relief. I was *in the future*—it still wasn't ideal, I didn't want this to be InterWorld's future, this crumbling ruin housing nothing but ashes and echoes, but it was better than it happening in my lifetime. For me, anyway. I kept reading.

Placing a trigger on this message—if you are reading it, you've found Captain Harker's office. Don't know what IW will be like in the future. Get to the port room if you can. Sending something to help. Can only guess your location in time. Don't touch anything else!

Good luck,

Josetta

I took a breath, waiting, but nothing else happened. After a moment, the letters faded; I touched the desk again, with the exact same result, the exact same words. So it wasn't "real time," as it were—it was literally a prerecorded script. Josetta must have used the tracer when I didn't come back, and set up the message and trigger for me. My only real concern was how long it had been until she decided to look for me. . . .

I looked down at the papers again, still tempted to try finding that picture . . . but Josetta had said not to touch anything, and I wasn't entirely sure she'd have a way of knowing whether I had or not. I left the room the way it was.

The port room was, as mentioned, all the way to the left of InterWorld. The Old Man's office was at the center, just about; I could make it there in ten minutes, four if I ran. I wondered what she was sending me. Walkers couldn't time travel, and neither could InterWorld itself—and even if it could, it certainly couldn't travel to itself in the future. I couldn't use the port room to warp back from here to there, could I?

"Even if I could, the ship is powered down," I muttered to myself, feeling a little better as the silence was broken.

I wasn't too worried about anything finding me; the entire base was silent and still, and I'd been trained nine ways from Sunday on the importance of heightened senses and being aware of your surroundings. I was alone on a dead world, one that used to be my home.

I couldn't help wondering if there were other messages for me, scattered throughout the world or on the other ships. Probably not, now that I thought of it. Josetta would have known the first place I'd go was the Old Man's office. Not only was it instinct, it was protocol. Still, I was curious about what had happened here—and as an agent of InterWorld, wasn't it my duty to find out? Maybe we could put precautions in place, something to stop this . . .

"But she said not to touch anything." I was picking my way through a hall that must have been used as a choke point for whatever had attacked them—us—though there were no bodies of any kind. Despite all the signs of struggle and Josetta's message, I hadn't encountered a single piece of evidence that anything living had *ever* been here. I didn't know how to feel about that.

I thought of all the coffins outside, all those silver boxes that carried us home when we died, wherever home was. Maybe I should have looked inside. The thought gave me chills.

I was still a hall or two over from the port room when I stopped, my hand brushing against something tacked to the wall. I squinted; the light was dim here, only one crack letting the red sunset through, but I was able to make out the words *I'm sorry* written in big, bold letters. I stared at them, at the paper taped haphazardly to the wall, and as my eyes adjusted I saw another. It said nothing, but had an artistic drawing of a redheaded, freckle-faced girl. A necklace hung next to it, dangling half over an embroidered napkin.

The red light from outside hit a bit of reflective metal, brightening the hallway just slightly. More notes, scraps of fabric, and other miscellaneous items dotted this wall, and I realized it wasn't a wall but the Wall, still being added to all these years—centuries—later.

The Wall. I just stared, taking in the faces of these Walkers who were dead and hadn't even been born yet, already nothing more than memories even though I'd never known them.

And then I realized I was still five halls from the infirmary, where the Wall had started. I wasn't even past the lockers yet, and the Wall had stretched this far. And if it had grown on the other side, too . . .

I wanted to protect them all, these heroes I'd never meet, these children who were just like me. I wanted to save them. I promised to the empty air that I would, somehow. Someday.

A flash of light filled the hall for a moment, affording me a view of the Wall in all its glory. Then it faded, and I was left in darkness more pronounced than it had been before.

That flash, brief as it had been, had ruined my night vision. I squinted, ducking down against the wall, my eyes on the far door. That had most likely been my helpful whatever-it-was from Josetta, though I was expecting her to send me an object—and my senses were telling me there was movement here now, something that wasn't me. I wished I had a blaster. Or an emitter. I'd have settled for a sharp stick at this point.

The dust motes visible in the fading light swirled in agitation as something moved in the doorway, a dark shape I could only partially see. I stayed absolutely still, watching and waiting as it hovered in the darkness, then bobbed forward—and then I recognized it.

"Hue!" I'd never been so glad to see anything in my life. My little mudluff friend brightened, becoming luminescent in the dimness; it was like having a balloon that also happened to be a lamp.

I ran forward, unabashedly throwing my arms around him, but he squeezed through my grasp, turning an apologetic powder blue. All but part of him, actually—there was a patch about the size of my hand that remained reddish, unchanged despite his other colors. If he were human, I'd've said it looked like a burn.

"Are you hurt, Hue?" He bobbed slightly, then stretched out a little, as he'd done in the In-Between when he'd protected me from J/O's laser. "Oh . . . I'm sorry, buddy. You saved me, though." He turned a pleased pink—all but that one patch—and started to bob back down the hall toward the port room.

"Where are you going?" He stopped, bobbed again, then continued, obviously expecting me to follow. I hesitated. "Are you taking me back to InterWorld? I mean, my InterWorld?" He brightened. I hesitated.

I wanted to go back, believe me. I wanted to erase the memory of this broken, falling-down base, go back to the reality of my classes and my little dorm room and my classmates. I wanted to see the mess hall all lit up, even if it was full of Walkers asking me about my *girlfriend*—which she sure as hell wasn't now—but as surely as I knew I wanted to go back, I also knew I couldn't. Not yet.

"Wait, Hue. I can't go back there yet." He paused, hovering uncertainly. If I went back, they'd detain and question me. They'd ask where I'd gone and why, and I'd have to explain about Acacia, and I wasn't sure *what* I could tell them about Jay. I wasn't even sure what I could tell them about Acacia.

"Acacia said it isn't safe there," I hedged, trying for a version of the truth. Hue flickered uncertainly. "I don't know why, but I have to find out. I have to go where she is. You can do that, can't you? That's why Josetta sent you to me. You're a multidimensional life-form, and the In-Between exists in all times. Time is a dimension, too, in that sense. It was the first place Acacia ever took me. The In-Between, in a different time. Can you get there, too?"

Colors were swirling uncertainly across Hue's surface, and I got the impression he was thinking. "I know Josetta told you to bring me back, but she doesn't know what's going on. There's danger there, and I don't know what it is. I have to find Acacia so she can tell me." That was only mostly true. I certainly didn't want to go back to TimeWatch, but anything was better than InterWorld—then *or* now. I couldn't help anyone if I was thrown in jail or kicked out again. Once I got to the In-Between, I'd . . . well, I'd think of something.

"Please, Hue?" The colors swirled faster, mingling into a muddy brown that slowly shifted to a lighter red. He wasn't happy about this, but he'd do it. I hoped.

His form shifted, becoming less spherical and more . . . liquid. He filtered down to the floor, crawling across it to my feet, and sort of . . . stretched up over me. I was reminded of when I'd put on Jay's encounter suit, after he'd died. I'd been afraid, then, as it swarmed up over my body; I was less afraid now because I knew Hue, because I trusted him, but it was still unnerving.

It felt like someone was covering me in Silly Putty, if you can imagine that. Or like being painted on, except he wasn't cold or anything. He was no temperature at all, which just contributed to the oddness.

I looked toward the Wall as Hue surged over my shoulders, my neck, my mouth. The sun had crept down past the jagged window, the last dying rays illuminating the first note I'd seen. *I'm sorry*, I thought as the world around me faded. *I'm so sorry*.

In retrospect, it may have been smarter to go back to Inter-World. I might have been detained for questioning, but at least I could have gotten some more equipment. I'd been traipsing about the Altiverse without even so much as a one-shot blaster glove for the last few days, and I was getting really tired of having to improvise weapons. I likely wouldn't have been as irritated if there'd been any weapons around for me *to* improvise with, but currently, the best I had was a wooden chair.

"You have to go!" Acacia shouted again, still struggling to free herself from the wires wrapping themselves around her. "Get out of here!"

Though I'd expected Hue to just carry me through the In-Between, to teleport me or whatever he'd done to save me from HEX, nothing had happened when he'd fully enveloped me. Well, nothing except for the fact that I could *see the zepto-seconds*. It was like looking through a kaleidoscope that made string theory look like connect the dots. He wasn't leading me so much as he was allowing me to see the path. And I'd found, while Hue was wrapped around me like a second skin, that I could Walk *anywhere*. Time, space, relativity—it was all the same, just a hop, skip, and a jump away.

I'd looked back and seen time, seen where I belonged, and leaped millennia in a single bound. It felt like taking my first steps.

I'd had the impression of InterWorld—not like I was actually flying over it, but just like I *knew* it was there, I was aware of it, like when you know without looking that someone's standing next to you. I knew it was there and full of me, full of my para-incarnations, but it was hazy. Something hung over it, a miasma I'd felt before, when my team and I had been captive on the *Malefic,* when we'd found the souls of dead Walkers, trapped in jars and powering the ship. . . .

The energy crackled in the air like static, and I could follow it. Like a hound tracing a scent, I followed it back to its source. I should have known it all along.

Earth $F\Delta98^6$. Where we'd "rescued" Joaquim.

He was already there when I Walked in, power swirling around him like electricity. We were in the very same room we'd rescued him from; he was standing near the window Jo had crashed through to get them to safety, some strange kind of energy vibrating in the air. The entire building was pulsing like a heartbeat, like a thousand heartbeats.

"Hi, Joey," he'd said with a smile, and then I'd seen Acacia.

She was restrained by wires and circuitry, held tightly against the far wall and looking like she'd seen better days. I'd seen her because she'd called out, her voice far stronger than she looked. It was probably the anger that gave her strength.

"Joe-what-the-*hell*-are-you-doing-here?" It was almost all one word, discernible only by the slight emphasis on my name and the mild expletive.

Well, if being pissed at me was helping keep her conscious, I was more than willing to play along. I wasn't too pleased with her either, frankly.

"Just trying to find out why you betrayed me, *Casey*. Seems to be a lot of that going around." I glanced at Joaquim, who frowned.

"I'm sorry." Joaquim said, then turned as Acacia began to struggle and spew curses. "Please be quiet," he said politely, though it was followed by a pulse of energy from the wires. She did, though not until after giving a strangled, pained noise that made my stomach constrict in sympathy. It was about right then that I started wishing I'd stopped to get a weapon.

Hue was no longer wrapped around me; I was vaguely aware of his presence, though I couldn't see him anywhere. All I had on me was the shield disk—fully charged still, since I hadn't used it for anything save my attempted escape from TimeWatch, and we remember how well that went—and the flag I'd intended to give as tribute to Jerzy's Wall. Joaquim, however, was armed with a blaster and that weird miasma thing surrounding him. It looked a little like a nebula—like he was standing in the middle of a star field, but there was something too sinister about it to be beautiful. It was familiar but subtly terrifying—like a nightmare you've had ever since you were a kid, the one you can't quite remember until you're almost asleep. I wasn't sure what it could do other than make my skin crawl, but I wasn't looking forward to finding out.

"I'm really glad you're not actually one of us," I told him, trying to ignore the way Acacia was struggling to raise her head again. "I didn't like you from the beginning."

"Basic Training section three oh one: Improvisational Tactics for Hostage Situations, chapter two, Emotional Warfare—try to get a rise out of your opponent." He smiled, looking both apologetic and horribly, infuriatingly smug. I hoped I never looked like that when I felt smug. "I am one of you, Joey."

"You can't be. I'd never betray us!" There was more I'd been intending to say, but he laughed, cutting me off.

"Yes, you would. If you had reason enough, if you knew it was the only way—you would, in a second."

"Never," I said passionately, though the tiniest bit of doubt made itself known in my mind. I would never hurt any of my para-incarnations or InterWorld—but would I betray them to save them, if I had to? I honestly didn't know—but I argued anyway, anger burning white-hot in my stomach. All his kind words about believing me, about wanting to hurry up and work with the team . . . "You *can't* be one of us. One of us could never betray us. We'd *know*. We'd *feel* it. We're not just cousins or siblings, we're . . ." I struggled to find something poetic to say, something that would drive the point home, but he was laughing. He was laughing, and it was hard to hold on to that belief when all the evidence to the contrary was right there in front of me.

"Are you trying to convince *me? Sense it*, Joey. I am one of you—you can feel it." He smiled again, spreading his arms and taking a step toward me—and this is where the scene started, with Acacia shouting for me to go. I mentioned I had a wooden chair, right? That's because they were next to the window, and so was Joaquim, and the window was still shattered from our daring "rescue."

I activated my shield disk, sprinting toward him. He half turned, stretching out a hand, and Acacia shouted again. I'd assumed he'd go for his blaster, but all he did was smirk at me, the star field coalescing around his fingers, sparking in the palm of his hand. I felt hot all over, but whatever he'd done didn't stop me. I grabbed up a chair and swung it full force as I ran. It hit him square on, knocking him clear off his feet and out the window behind him. I was just sorry the glass had already been shattered. That would have been more satisfying, though it did give me something I could use to free Acacia.

I ran over to her, slicing at the wires with a long shard of glass. Some of them were thick cables, others were just telephone wire; those cut easily and she was able to wriggle free.

I somehow expected a thank-you or at least a nod, maybe, before she started telling me what to do.

I didn't expect a slap in the face.

"What was that for?"

"Calling me Casey," she snapped, but then she hugged me. I didn't really have time to enjoy it, since I was still reeling from the slap and she only had her arms around me for a second before she pulled back, looking like she might slap me again. "You weren't supposed to be here, I *told you* to—"

"You didn't tell me *anything*, Acacia. You stabbed me in the back and kidnapped me, not to mention *stranding* me—"

"I didn't stab you," she protested.

"Semantics! You still—"

"It doesn't matter, will you just *shut up* for a—"

"Aren't you two *adorable*?" Joaquim's voice rang out, louder and somehow . . . fuller than it had been before. The hair on the back of my neck stood up as the room filled with power, a wind picking up from seemingly nowhere. I automatically got in front of Acacia—she elbowed me in the ribs, which were still bruised and aching, thank you very much—and shifted around to stand next to me. We both looked to the window.

Joaquim was just outside it, and he was sort of . . . flying. Well, hovering. He was suspended in midair just outside the window, hundreds of little blue sparks flying around him so quickly it looked like he had a force field of some kind. They reflected in the shattered glass still clinging to the window frame and on the floor, creating a dizzying whirlwind of light, like he was the center of a solar system.

"Poor Captain Harker," Joaquim said, still just . . . *hanging* out there, in the air. "He misses you terribly sometimes," he told Acacia, his expression turning, for a moment, genuinely sympathetic. "I don't blame him, knowing what will happen."

I glanced at Acacia, looking for some sort of recognition or understanding. She just looked uncertain.

"What are you talking about?" she said. "You can't possibly know the future—you're just a Walker."

Affronted as I was by the *just a Walker* comment, I was equally affronted that she'd make that statement about Joaquim. "He's not a Walker."

"Wrong," Joaquim said. "Both of you. You're both wrong. I have the energy of Captain Joseph Harker flowing through me, and that includes some of his memories. You were very dear to him, you know."

Acacia remained silent, stunned and uncertain, but I wasn't paying attention to her. I wasn't paying attention to Joaquim anymore, either. I was looking at the little blue lights, the whirlwind of static and emotion surrounding him. I was feeling the way the wind was warm and sparking with purpose. I was remembering the last time I'd seen little blue lights like that, and I was suddenly sick with *knowing*.

I was looking at the souls of dead Walkers.

CHAPTER FOURTEEN

"ARE YOU FEELING OKAY, Joey? You look a little dizzy." It was hard to tell whether he was being snide or genuine, but I really didn't care.

"You're making me sick," I tried, but the truth was I *felt* a little dizzy. I was too warm, and my limbs were too heavy. I was tired, and reeling from the knowledge that Joaquim wasn't *one of us*, he was *all of us*. All the Walkers who've ever been captured . . .

"You finally get it." He was still smiling at me, the little blue lights—the *souls*—whirling around him and carrying him back through the shattered window. His feet touched the ground and the souls stopped whirling so fast, though there was still a spark in the air, a muted excitement. *We're free*, they exulted. *Use us! We can help!* I wondered if they even knew what they were being used *for*, that they were made to be traitors just like him. I doubted there was enough of them left to know.

"Where did you get them?" I edged my feet a little further apart, trying to regain my center of gravity. The floor seemed to be rolling beneath me just a little, like I was on a ship amid a calm sea. HEX kept their Walkers captive in jars, after they'd boiled them down to their very essences . . . but we weren't dealing with HEX now; this was Binary. Unmistakably so. Binary carbon-froze the Walkers they caught, plugged them into something like a giant battery, and used their energy that way. Could Joaquim have once *been* a Walker? I wasn't sure that was possible. . . .

"Everywhere." Joaquim spread his arms to either side, his gaze seeming to burn through mine. "Here and there, all of space and time. Anywhere a Walker's died, with the technology of Binary and—"

"Enough, child." Next to me, Acacia turned—and I felt her go rigid, though I couldn't quite muster the energy to turn and look. In a moment I didn't have to, for the figure came into my view.

I'd been face-to-face with Lord Dogknife, the leader of HEX. I'd stared right at him and somehow hadn't flinched, even when I'd smelled dead things on his breath and seen maggots crawling across his teeth. I'd looked him in the eye and demanded he give me what I wanted, and what was more, I'd gotten out of it alive. I'm not bragging; I need you to understand what I mean when I say I shouldn't have been afraid of this man.

He wasn't very tall, and looked kind of like a cross between your dorky science teacher and the small kid who always gets picked last for the team. He wore clunky brown shoes and completely unwrinkled tan pants, a tweed jacket, and a bow tie. And Coke-bottle glasses. And behind those glasses, there was nothing but static.

I'm serious. You know how when your cable TV is disconnected and there's nothing but static on the screen? You know how they use it for horror movies all the time, with people seeing things in it? His eyes were like that. No pupils, nothing. Just static.

I could still tell he was looking at me.

"Yes, Professor." Joaquim's voice cut smoothly through the hypnotic effect of those eyes, and I blinked rapidly. My eyes burned like I'd been staring at a computer screen for hours.

Professor. This was the Professor. 01101. Leader of the Binary.

Behind us, through the door the Professor had come in from, a dozen or so Binary clones took up position around the room. The Professor regarded us, the tweed and glasses and bow tie all striking me as absurdly unfunny.

"Have you finished draining him yet?"

"Not yet, Professor. I've made the connection."

He nodded. Just . . . nodded. And looked at me. And waited.

It clicked. I knew why I felt weak, and why Joaquim had the Old Man's memories, and what he'd done to me earlier, before I'd knocked him through the window. I knew what he'd been about to say before the Professor had interrupted him—and remembering the dry, rust-colored soil that had been cleaned of any trace of blood, I was desperately, fervently hoping I wasn't right.

"You're a clone," I told Joaquim, and I had the small satisfaction of seeing him pause. He glanced at the Professor, then at me, uncertainty showing on his face. "You were grown by Binary, in a vat, just like the vegetables." I nodded to the scouts.

"And infused with the souls of your kind," the Professor agreed. Joaquim was just looking at me.

A thick, cold knot of dread was settling like a rock in my stomach, warring only with the white-hot anger I felt at knowing they'd used Jay's blood. If I was right about that, there was only one explanation for how a Binary-grown clone had the powers and abilities of a Walker. It defied all reason, everything I'd been taught—and at the same time, made perfect, horrible sense. "And HEX's magic."

"What?" Acacia's voice was barely a whisper.

"You're working with HEX," I nerved myself and looked at the Professor, though I couldn't meet those static eyes for long. "You grew him, they powered him."

"And *gave* me power," Joaquim snapped, and I almost fell

to my knees at the surge of weakness that washed over me. "They gave me the power to fix everything."

Acacia's hand found mine, though I wasn't sure if she was scared or warning me about something. Neither, apparently—I saw a flash in my peripheral vision, and a jolt went up through my arm. There was the sound that was half static shock and half something snapping, and Joaquim reeled back slightly. I suddenly felt a ton better. Acacia had broken whatever link Joaquim had made with me.

I should have used that moment to do something, but I was too stunned, too unprepared, and too paralyzed with the knowledge I'd just discovered. Binary and HEX . . . the war for supremacy between them had been one of the only things giving InterWorld a much-needed edge. They were *working together* now. We'd just lost our only advantage.

Put succinctly, we were screwed.

The Professor looked at Acacia—just looked at her, nothing else—and she cried out like she'd been electrocuted, slumping to the ground.

I caught her halfway down, and I think I said her name. She didn't respond; her eyes were open, but she didn't seem to be conscious. I could feel her breathing, but she didn't react to me at all.

"Drain him," said the Professor, but Joaquim hesitated.

"It would take me a while. He's strong."

"Then bring him. The girl, too." He was still talking to

Joaquim, but the clones moved forward to grab us. I fought to hold on to Acacia, but she was still unresponsive and there were far more of them than there were of me. Joaquim grinned at me.

"You and me, Joey. The heralds of FrostNight."

One of the clones clubbed me in the back of the head, hard, and the next few moments were a haze of hallways and doors while I tried stubbornly to hold on to consciousness. Joaquim's words rattled around in my head as the clones dragged me through the halls—*FrostNight*. I'd heard that before. I'd heard someone say that before . . .

FrostNight comes.

The words had been whispered, pained. There had been blood on the rocky ground. He'd looked at me, and warned me, and died.

Jay . . .

Despite my attempts to stay conscious, I must have passed out for a few moments at least. When my vision cleared I was in some sort of cage. I didn't see Acacia anywhere, but Joaquim was next to me.

No—it wasn't a cage, exactly. I was surrounded by metal, but it was more than that. It was mesh, see-through, but vaguely human shaped. There was a rounded part for my head and room for my arms, which were stretched out to either side of me. My hands were trapped, my wrists stuck through padded restraints that felt like the cuffs used to check blood pressure. They were around my ankles, too, and hundreds of little multicolored wires were twined and twisted out of them. There were straps about my chest, waist, and legs. I could turn my head but not move my body.

Thin, prickly fingers of dread began to clutch at my stomach. This was it. I was strapped in so tightly I couldn't even feel my fingers, InterWorld was most likely on full lockdown due to Joaquim's slow drain, Hue was still only a dim presence in the back of my mind, and Acacia was unconscious or worse. I was trapped by Binary, and nothing short of a miracle was going to get me out.

Joaquim was strapped in as well, and didn't seem at all concerned. "You made this possible, you know," he said, as though I were helping him complete his life's work. Which, however unwilling I was, may have been the case. "It would have taken me days, weeks even, to pull all the power from InterWorld. I couldn't do it all at once. There are too many of us. Slowly, yes . . . But *you*, Joey. You're one of the most powerful Walkers they have. Without you, this would have taken *months* . . ."

I wanted to ask what *this* was. I wanted to ask why he was strapped in, too. I wanted to ask what this was going to do, or why he was so happy about it. I wanted to panic, and struggle, and yell. Instead, I mumbled "Where's Acacia?" and made a serious attempt at lifting my head to look around.

"Your concern is sweet, it really is. I hope I feel love, someday. I did get along well with Joliette. I'm glad she survived the rockslide. I'd hoped everyone would . . . but it had to be done."

It had to be done. Of course Joaquim had caused the rockslide. He'd needed the base on lockdown, needed everyone inside so he could drain as many of them as possible. Everything clicked, now; the fog hanging over Base Town after Jerzy's death, what I'd assumed to be depression . . . it had been a tangible thing. Jo's lethargy after she and Joaquim had made it back to Base—that's how he'd even gotten the InterWorld formula in the first place, made it through the In-Between. He'd stolen her energy, and her memories, and Walked right into InterWorld like some kind of goddamned hero.

And we'd let him.

As near to panic as I'd been a moment ago, a sudden calm settled over me now. I ignored him, turning my attention to getting feeling back into my extremities. I'd need to have full use of all my limbs if I was going to attempt a daring escape, after all—not that I had a plan, mind you. I had nothing but the burning need to not let the traitor who shared my face get away with Jerzy's death.

I flexed the fingers of my right hand, then my left, finally managing to work some blood back into them. That was good, but it was accompanied by a severe case of pins and needles;

I let that sort itself out while I tried to discern exactly what kind of contraption I was in.

The wires went from me and Joaquim down into a bundle on the ground and out past our feet. They snaked across the floor—which seemed to have a bunch of symbols etched into it, arcane-looking things that were straight out of a B-movie cult flick—and split off into different directions, weaving and interlocking to create a five-pointed star. Just above the star was the oddest machine I'd ever seen.

I recognized some of it, thanks to my studies at Inter-World—transmitters, receptors, generators, amplifiers—they were all jumbled together surrounding something that looked almost like a giant Tesla coil. Looking vastly out of place amid all the machinery were figures in dark robes, nothing but blackness visible beneath their hoods. There were thirteen of them, just standing there, all in a circle around the coil.

No, thank you. Whatever this was, I didn't want any part of it.

Now that I was a little calmer, I closed my eyes, casting about for a portal . . . and immediately wrenched my awareness back to the safety of my own mind. There were *things* out there, things that were aware of me, that knew I was trying to Walk. . . . It felt like I'd passed through a spiderweb or gotten too close to a live wire. The hair on the back of my neck stood up.

"It should be soon," Joaquim murmured, and I finally turned my attention back to him.

"Okay, I'll bite. FrostNight—what *is* it? I was warned about it, by—by an old friend," I said quickly, but Joaquim gave a sympathetic nod.

"Jay," he said, and I realized the calm anger that had settled over me before was *nothing* compared to what I was feeling now. The thought of Jay's spirit being used for something like this . . . But, no, these were only the souls of captured Walkers. I had brought Jay's body back to Inter-World, seen him off, spoken with his spirit. Jay was safe, and so was Jerzy.

Joaquim confirmed this a second later, though I was still too angry to care much for the understanding in his voice. "I have some of your memories, too, Joey. Only a few—we weren't linked long enough for me to get much more."

"Well, I don't have yours," I snapped. "So enlighten me. What's FrostNight?"

"The revolution that will reshape everything," Joaquim said simply, with the kind of rapture you find only among zealots and fools.

"Okay," I prompted when he ceased to say more, keeping his attention on my face while I wiggled my right arm back and forth. My wrist was beginning to chafe, but I thought it was starting to come free a little. Maybe. I hoped.

"FrostNight. The Ragnarok Wave. Armageddon, if you

want to be dramatic. It's a soliton. A self-aware explosion that will reshape time and space."

The sudden, overwhelming disgust I felt was doing wonders to distract me from the feel of my wrist chafing against my bonds. "So you're helping them destroy the universe. Can you *get* any more cliché? Why don't villains ever want something rational?"

Joaquim smirked at me. "When did I *ever* say it would destroy the universe? I said it would *reshape* time and space. We can make the universe, the Altiverse, whatever we choose. We are destroying nothing. We're *re-creating*."

Somehow, that was worse.

"Okay," I said slowly, trying to work all this out. "So you're *re-creating* the universe. Why? Isn't it fine the way it is?"

"Not hardly. Look at the horrors we've seen, that *I've* seen, just in the few days I was on InterWorld! The more I was educated there, the more I learned, the more I realized our mission *had* to succeed. The memories I touched on only reinforced this—so much grief, so much anger, so much tragedy. So much chaos . . ."

"*Joaquim*. This is *basic common sense*—without bad things, there's no way to quantify good!"

"Poetic philosophy," he snapped back. "I wonder if all of us would agree. Do you know how many of us were hurt? Abused?"

I didn't know, and I didn't *want* to know. All of my

para-incarnations were born from para-incarnations of my parents, and I just couldn't believe that even alternate world versions of my affectionate mother and cheerful father could hurt their kids.

As if following my train of thought—which was possible, since he was technically my clone and shared a similar brain structure—Joaquim continued with: "My father and mother have envisioned a better universe for us, one where we can enforce peace and order."

Hold the phone. "Your father and mother? You're a *clone*."

"I was given life, same as you. By Binary, and HEX."

"That's a hell of a family," I muttered, and I think I actually made him angry.

"My parents are reshaping the entire Altiverse for me! Would yours do the same?"

"No, because mine are *sane*."

"*Joe!*"

I felt a shock go through me—that was Acacia. I looked around wildly, trying to find her. A laser blast went off somewhere to my right; a second later I saw one of those blobs of mercury the Binary clones shoot zing past my cage. Acacia was fighting them—all of them—using a combination of martial arts and various gadgets from her belt.

"Joe, *Walk*!" she screamed. "*Now! You have to Walk!*"

Joaquim spoke up serenely from my side. "They're ready."

The machines flared to life around me, and I couldn't

have Walked even if I was willing to leave Acacia. It felt like I was in the core of a jet turbine, and everything I knew about Walking—or about anything, for that matter—was spinning around inside my head like that teacups ride at Disneyland. For a second I didn't know where or even who I was, and then Acacia screamed my name again and I heard chanting start up from around the circuitry star. I couldn't understand what they were saying, but for all I knew they could have been speaking English. I probably wouldn't have comprehended the alphabet right then.

Joaquim looked like he was on a roller coaster, eyes alight, more animated than I'd ever seen him, even though we were both strapped to whatever kind of conductor this was. The blue lights—the souls—that had been dancing around him were gone.

No, not gone. The wires that fed from his machine were glowing blue, and I could hear them. Over the chanting, over the sound of the engines and the machines, I could hear them.

They were screaming.

The light was flowing through the wires to the Tesla-coil thing, and a sphere was slowly growing above it. It was misty, ice blue, and roiling like it contained a storm. There was another sphere surrounding it, fed by the power of the thirteen robed chanters. They were containing it, whatever "it" was. *FrostNight comes . . .*

Abruptly, it all stopped. The last of the blue light was sucked into the growing sphere, and the robed figures changed their chant. I was still reeling. I felt like part of my soul had just been sucked out, but at least now I could understand what they were saying.

"By science and magic begotten, by sorcery contained and technology bonded—"

It didn't sound good.

Joaquim was not nearly as excited now. His head drooped as though too heavy to hold up, his skin was pale and clammy looking. As bad as that had been for me, I didn't feel nearly as weak as he looked.

He lifted his head, that small motion obviously taking a lot out of him. "Professor . . ." He sounded scared. I admit I actually felt for him; there was a slowly awakening comprehension in his eyes that chilled me to my core. "Professor!"

The leader of Binary was nowhere to be seen. There were only the robed and hooded figures, still chanting, the clones standing guard and the ones who'd finally managed to subdue Acacia. She was no longer struggling; instead, she was looking up at the growing orb of energy with the same kind of horror Joaquim was starting to show.

The thirteen figures raised their arms, lowering them all at once; and some of the clones, standing next to various bits of machinery near the walls, turned to press or pull buttons or switches. The wires flared to life again, and Joaquim started to struggle.

"*Professor!*" he screamed, his voice barely audible above the whirring of machinery, the nightmarish chanting. "*Professor, what is this?*"

I knew why he was panicking. It felt like I was being drained of blood drop by drop, like every bit of haecceity was being sucked from me and replaced with empty promises, echoes of what I'd once been. It only took me a moment to recognize the feeling. I'd felt that empty after the Old Man had drained my memories, took my ability to Walk. . . . I'd been fine most days, but lying there in the silence of my room, I'd often cried and wondered why. It was because he'd taken everything I *was* from me.

"Be still," the Professor's voice commanded, carrying easily above the din though he was still nowhere to be seen. "This was the intent behind your creation, Joaquim. You will fulfill your purpose and bring about the revolution of the world."

"*No!*" he screamed, his struggling becoming wilder. "*I don't want to—*"

There was a flare of blue, so bright I had to shut my eyes, though it was gone immediately after. The machinery around us crackled, and the acrid smell of smoke reached my nose. The transmitter nearest Joaquim was on fire. Some of the clones, acting on an unspoken signal, rushed over to put it out—but Joaquim was still struggling, his body enveloped in blue, the fuses short-circuiting one by one. In his eyes was the same fear I'd felt a dozen times since I'd come to Inter-World. It was the fear of death.

"*Joe!*" Acacia screamed from somewhere to my right. "*Help him!*"

Help him? I didn't know how to help him—what could I possibly do to help him? And more important, why would I? He was nothing more than a Binary clone, imbued with power stolen from Walkers—

The cords attached to Joaquim were sparking, pulsing as he struggled. With a strength born of desperation, he ripped one arm free of the bindings, reaching toward me. He looked terrified.

Though my arm was chafed nearly from knuckles to elbow, I'd managed to wiggle enough that I slipped my arm from the cuff that'd held me. That same calm I'd felt before, when he'd mentioned the rockslide, was wrapped around me like a blanket. I knew what to do.

With every ounce of willpower I possessed, I wrenched the remains of my power from the wires, from the fuses and the massive orb pulsing greedily in the center of the room. I called it back to me, commanded it, and grabbed Joaquim's hand. The blue glow spread to envelop me, whispers and pleas brushing against my mind. *Use us*, they said. *Free us. Let us Walk again.*

I closed my eyes, found the core of power inside me, centered myself, as I'd been taught—and let it explode outward, focused on the fuses around me. The chanting was momentarily lost in the sound of electricity, of the wires crackling and popping. I used the souls as Joaquim had done, directing them to burn through my bonds. It was so easy.

I was standing now, no longer caged, no longer captive. I was the eye of the storm, immune to the chaos around me. The chanting, the fires, the fuses—none of it touched me. The clones fired at me, and I activated my shield disk with a mere thought, the projectiles sliding right off me to thunk to the floor. I was aware of the entire room, the ebb and flow of the energy, the people in it. FrostNight, ever growing, greedily absorbing the power of the Walkers.

And a portal. Here. *Now.*

I stretched out a hand to Acacia, still held by the Binary clones. *Free her.*

The little blue lights arced from my fingers like stars, like fireworks, flying toward Acacia. Each of them touched a clone, and one by one, they were zapped into nothing. I didn't stop to watch any further. They would do as I asked, I was sure of it. I turned back to Joaquim and the machine, stretching out my other hand. The blue lights hesitated. *Help him*, I directed, but they faltered.

"Joe!" Acacia was beside me now, one hand clutching my wrist. "You can't save him, we have to Walk—"

"*You* told me to help him!" I shrugged her off, taking a few steps toward the machines. Joaquim was looking at me, eyes wide and frightened, his free hand reaching out, desperately trying to close the distance between us.

"To get you out of the machine, to take his power back—"

Anger flared suddenly, deep in my chest. She'd told me to help him only to *use* him? No—we were better than that. We had to be. *I* had to be.

I stumbled away from her, moving toward Joaquim and the machine. One step closer, two—three—

"You *can't*!" She threw her arms around my neck, using her weight to slow me. I faltered as she pressed against my fractured shoulder, still not healed from the rockslide Joaquim had caused. Electricity was crackling in the air all around us, the power undulating, vibrating back and forth, bouncing all around the room. The thirteen figures stood untouched around the circuitry star, arms at their sides, the chanting once again in a language even I, with all my Inter-World training, couldn't understand. Whatever they were doing, they didn't seem concerned with us; the little blue lights were winking out, one by one. I couldn't tell if they were being freed or dying.

"It's almost complete," Acacia pleaded into my ear, her broken nails digging into my shoulder and chest. "*You're* powering it, you and him, *right now*—"

"Then we should get him out—"

"You can't, Joe, it's too late! He doesn't have his own essence—he's a consciousness powered by dead things and they've left him—"

"He's a consciousness," I yelled back, ripping away from her. I took two steps toward Joaquim, before I stopped in my tracks. All around me, the wind was whipping and the fires were burning and the clones were being zapped to ashes by a hundred pieces of my soul, and through it all Joaquim was still reaching, still holding his hand out—but there was nothing there. There was nothing in his eyes anymore, not anger or hatred or fear. He wasn't looking at me, not really. He was looking through me. He was holding his hand out to the lights.

Acacia's hand slipped into mine. I couldn't look away from that face, my face, with the dead eyes.

"Walk, Joe," Acacia whispered, and somehow I heard her, even over the chaos surrounding us.

I swallowed, closing my eyes. *I'm sorry,* I thought at the lights, as I'd told the memories of their successors on the Wall, so many years in the future. *I'm so sorry.*

I took a breath, finding the gate in my mind. It opened, and I followed the path that was home, leaving the dead Walkers and the empty one behind.

CHAPTER FIFTEEN

OF THE DOZEN OR so prehistoric planets where InterWorld made its home, my favorite was still the first one I'd ever come to. I know it sounds odd to say, but it felt a little bit like *my* home—it was familiar, even though the landmarks in each world looked almost identical. Still, I don't care if it was just my imagination, just nostalgia for the first world I'd come to after I'd left mine. The sunsets always seemed rosier, the sunrises brighter, the sky bluer. Today was no exception as Acacia and I stood on a cliff overlooking a great valley, so close our clothing touched with every breeze. The valley was beautiful; the world around us was calm; the sun was setting.

We'd been standing there in silence for a few minutes, waiting for InterWorld to pick us up. There were tears on my face, and I didn't even care if she saw them.

"I know you wanted to save him," she said, not looking at me. "I'm sorry, Joe, I really am."

"What was that thing?"

". . . I don't know."

"You looked like you knew."

"I . . ." She looked away, which was impressive since she still hadn't been looking at me in the first place. "I don't know what it was, exactly. I know it was the most terrifying thing I've ever felt. It felt like it . . . could just erase me. And I can cast anchor to any time and place in the Altiverse, Joe. I can run as fast and as far as I need to." She paused for a moment, and her voice was very small when she spoke again. "I don't think I could run from that."

"He called it FrostNight," I said after a moment, watching a flock of birds skim along the surface of a small lake in the distance. "I was warned about it once before."

She shook her head. "I've never heard of it."

"Was it completed?" I asked, afraid of the answer. "You said we were powering it. Did they . . . ?"

"I don't know," she said again. "I don't . . . think so."

"We have to figure out what it does."

"We can go back to TimeWatch, search the archives—"

"No," I interrupted, turning my gaze to the sky. "We're going to report first." She was silent for another moment.

"I don't report to InterWorld, Joe." She sounded apologetic. I turned to face her, looking down into her eyes. I was just glad to see someone looking back at me.

"Doesn't mean you can't, Cay." Her brow furrowed slightly,

but she allowed the nickname, obviously considering this. "You were there, too. You saw everything happen. I'm . . ." Now I had to look away, swallowing hard against the sudden hopelessness that settled in the pit of my stomach. "I'm liable to get thrown out again if it's just me coming back with another crazy story. I've seen the deaths of two Walkers—three, if you count Joaquim. Hundreds more, if you count all those souls. I've seen the end of InterWorld, thanks to you." She drew in a breath, shifting slightly, but I kept on. "I signed out to go for a Walk, and accidentally brought on the thing I was warned about when I first arrived here, something that even scares a Time Agent and took the essences of a hundred of me to power. Just come report with me, okay?"

She was looking up at me, a maddening little smile starting to turn up the corners of her mouth. "So you're asking for my help."

"It's the least you can do for betraying me."

She paused. "Joe . . ."

"You were just trying to help me, I know."

"No, I was trying to *save* you. There was a massive power flux in InterWorld Prime that was—I know now—because of Joaquim. I didn't know who the traitor was, but I was going to have to bring the information that there *was* one to Captain Harker, and he was just as likely to suspect you as anyone. More so. That is even if he was able to do anything about it, and with the massive amount of power being channeled from them, I didn't think so."

"Joaquim had his memories," I said quietly, taking her hands. She let me, nodding. "It's because he was stealing them, right? Taking their power, like the machine tried to do to me?" She nodded again. "So they might all be—" The image of the InterWorld of the future flashed through my mind, abandoned and wrecked. . . .

"No, they're stable. I promise; they're all okay. They're just . . . I don't know that they're coming, Joe."

"Why not?"

"If you were Captain Harker, and you had a traitor on your ship slowly siphoning the energy from everyone on it, what would you do?"

"Find the traitor."

"What if he was gone by the time you found him? What if he'd taken what he needed and gotten away with it?"

"I'd try to break the link. I don't—" But then I did understand, all at once. I'd try to break the link. I'd throw the ship out of time, as quickly as possible, and get as far away from the receiver as possible. I'd punch it. And God help anyone left behind.

"They're not coming," I said. My voice sounded strange in my own ears.

"I'm sorry, Joe."

I kept silent, just standing there, holding her hands. There wasn't anything I could say.

had brought me home, but home was beyond my reach.

"Come to TimeWatch with me," she said, giving a light squeeze of my hands that brought my gaze back to her, however unwillingly. "As a guest. As a friend."

I stared at her for a moment, reading the earnest hope on her face, the desire to make me understand. "No cells?"

She smiled, brilliantly. "No cells. No holding fields, no Sentry."

"Oh, is that what they're called? The hulking men in the suits that look like secret service on steroids?"

She laughed, eyes sparkling. "The Sentry. He's our main guard."

"Your *main* guard? For all of TimeWatch?"

"He has more than one form."

"Do any of them speak with their mouths, or is that part of the intimidation factor?"

She laughed again. The idea of going with her was becoming more and more appealing.

She looked up at me and I looked down at her, and we were both smiling. "I like you better when you don't have to have the last word all the time," I told her, and she didn't even blink.

"I like you better when you aren't trying to impress me."

"Nah, I gave up on that when you stood up to the Old Man."

"He's not that scary."

I thought of the picture in the Old Man's desk, of him and the older her, of the way they'd been smiling. I wondered if she was going to be his someday, or if she already had been. I wondered if this technically counted as making moves on my boss's girl, but it was mattering less and less because she was tilting her face up toward me and our arms were around each other now, and I didn't know if I'd ever see the Old Man or InterWorld again.

I shouldn't have been surprised when something huge blocked out the sun right then, right when our faces were so close I could feel her breath. I shouldn't have been surprised when the ship blinked into existence right above us, but I was, and I was further surprised when I looked up and *it wasn't InterWorld*.

It was worse than the *Malefic* and that horrible FrostNight machine combined. It was bigger and darker than anything I'd ever seen, surrounded by a halo—no, a miasma—of tiny particles like Saturn's rings, except they were swirling and pivoting like a cloud of wasps around a disturbed nest. Worst of all, it was completely *silent*, like an animal stalking its prey.

I pulled Acacia back beneath a tree as the particles shifted and swirled, still absolutely silent, streams of them shooting out in all directions. In less than a minute they'd completely blanketed the sky, like storm clouds in winter.

We were afraid to even whisper, afraid to breathe. The

miasma grew denser and denser, until it was as dark as a moonless night, and the sky churned and roiled like a thing alive.

Then, high up and slightly to the side of us, there was an outline of something, a flicker, a shadow—then it was gone, and back, and gone again, but I'd seen the shape of it and it was one I knew as well as my own heart.

The black ship began to flicker as well, out of time with the other shape, and the particles were swirling faster and faster in the sky, shifting and whirling and writhing, twisting around the other. Slowly, they began to flicker in tandem.

HEX had found InterWorld—and something else had found us.

I whirled, my arms still wrapped around Acacia—but I couldn't protect her from the air, the miasma that permeated this entire area. I wasn't even sure what had struck her, but she gasped and went limp in my arms. I tried to hold on to her, as I had when we'd been separated by Binary, but something lashed out and hit me in my injured side. I doubled over; the only way I could save myself from a broken rib was to roll with it. The darkness grew thicker, more pronounced, and I lost sight of Acacia.

Shadows swept up in front of me, coalescing, forming strong hands that grabbed me by the throat. I felt my feet leave the ground as the darkness continued to take shape, forming into a figure from my nightmares.

Lord Dogknife.

"We meet again, pup." He smiled, the expression not at all pleasant. I didn't bother trying to break his grip; he was too strong for that. Instead, I snaked a hand down to my belt, going for my shield disk. I didn't know how much charge it had left or what it would do about his hand on my throat, if anything, but it was the best option I had right then.

He let go with one hand, claws grabbing my wrist before I could make it to the shield. His grip was hard, but what worried me more was the way his fur felt against my skin. It was warm and sticky, matted with a viscous substance I desperately hoped wasn't blood. I still couldn't see Acacia. I looked up, unable to do anything else, looked to the faint outline of my home as it flitted through the sky.

"Your ship isn't coming for you, child." His red eyes were wide, ears perked up with excitement. The expression closely mirrored a dog's in a way that was entirely unfunny; a sick parody of something usually comforting and familiar. "Poor little pup, abandoned by his pack . . . They couldn't come get you, even if they wanted to."

Finally, *finally*, I saw movement behind him. Acacia was struggling to her feet, using the wide tree trunk behind her as leverage. In one hand was the little beeper thingy she'd used to fire at J/O. She raised it and aimed—

Lord Dogknife whirled around, letting go of my throat. He lashed a hand out, smacking the weapon out of her hand

and knocking her to the ground. I caught a glimpse of her face as she fell; her nose was bleeding, eyes shutting tightly in pain.

He'd let go of me—that was something. I put all my weight on one leg, using his grip on my wrist as leverage, and sent my heel toward his face. He caught my ankle and pulled, slamming me back onto the ground. Sharp teeth glinting in a fierce, canine grin, he twisted my wrist in his strong grip. I felt something snap, and it took me a moment to realize the hoarse shout of pain had come from me.

"Your ship is stranded out of time, Walker," he whispered, his voice somewhere between a growl and a purr. "You are the last one left, and you should be commended. It was you who made all this possible."

I didn't know if he was just saying that to get a rise out of me, or if he really was evil to a cliché—I didn't care, at this point. I couldn't feel my fingers, and Acacia wasn't moving anymore. I wasn't sure if it was just the pain from my broken wrist making me dizzy, or if she was actually starting to glow. Certainly everything was looking a little fuzzy.

I tried to wriggle a leg up between us so I could kick him off me, start fighting again, but he was way too strong. His breath was rancid in my face, the sickeningly sweet smell of rotting meat.

"It was you who destroyed my ship, little Walker. And in doing so, showed me how to defeat you. We are even now, yes? I could kill you, little fly, but I have something far better in mind."

A small, tiny, faint glimmer of hope began to make itself known in my gut. If he wasn't going to kill me, whatever it was, I could get out of it. If he wanted to boil me down to my essence and try to capture my soul, I'd escaped from that before. I could handle that.

"Your death would be a kindness—you have already failed. You can Walk, but where will you go? You cannot return to your ship, and the few precious moments you have left will not be enough to stop us. FrostNight comes, little Walker. You have already seen it."

Something about the ground beneath me started to feel odd, like it was becoming softer—or I was sinking. I took my gaze away from his face long enough to glance down at the grass beneath me, and my eyes went wide.

It was wilting. As I watched, it turned brown and brittle, dying right beneath me. The smell of rotting debris was all around me, and I could hear insects buzzing around my eyes, could see flies dropping from the sky as they, too, died.

"The power that will reshape everything." His voice was echoing in my ears, everything around me sounding hollow. "FrostNight. The Ragnarok Wave. Our Silver Dream."

Darkness was creeping into the edges of my vision. At first I thought I was passing out, then I realized the ground was actually turning black.

"You will be alive to see it, little Walker. And you will not be able to Walk far enough away."

The ground gave way beneath me, and as I felt myself starting to fall, I saw Acacia's body glowing bright green. She shimmered and vanished, and I fell into the Nowhere-at-All.

EPILOGUE

I WAS THERE ONLY for a few moments, but it felt like forever. The Nowhere-at-All was as disorienting as the In-Between in its own way. Instead of everything, there was absolutely nothing. No sound, no light, no air—at least not at first. After you'd been there for a few seconds, you realized you weren't alone, that there were things in the darkness that knew exactly where *you* were.

The one time I'd been there before, I'd managed to will myself where I needed to be. I tried to focus enough to do that now, but I was in too much pain—too tired, too worried, too scared. And too lost. I didn't know where I was going, but I knew it couldn't be to InterWorld. I couldn't get home.

Just as I was wondering if Lord Dogknife's plan had been to trap me in the Nowhere-at-All forever—an admittedly terrifying thought—I saw a small dot in the distance. It grew as I felt toward it, becoming so bright I had to close my eyes. As soon as I did, it was as though I suddenly gained both weight and mass, and was free-falling to my death. I had time for about two seconds of abject panic before I hit the ground.

Surprisingly, it didn't hurt—not much, anyway. Though it felt like I'd been falling forever, I'd hit the ground from maybe two, three feet up.

Yes, the ground. It smelled like dirt and grass, and when I opened my eyes, that's exactly what was beneath me.

I groaned, rolling over onto my side. My wrist hurt like nothing else I'd ever experienced—even my fractured shoulder during the avalanche—and I was sure that one of my ribs was actually broken this time. I was alone . . . back on the world I'd just come from? No . . . I could hear something in the distance, a familiar sound. Ships?

No.

Something else.

I sat up, looking with disbelief to one side of me, where the machines sped along in neat rows.

Cars.

I managed to get to my feet, making my way toward them. I was in a park—and that bench looked familiar. So did that stone statue. The street signs were names I recognized.

I was home. Not InterWorld Base Town—*home*. My home. My world.

Lord Dogknife had not only left me alive, he'd sent me *home*.

FrostNight comes, his voice whispered in my mind. *And you will be alive to see it, little Walker.*

The power that will reshape everything. . . .

Binary and HEX wanted to reshape the Altiverse, to gain complete control. To make all worlds into what they wished. He had sent me home, but soon, there wouldn't be a home. It would be erased, and I along with it.

I limped toward the intersection, breathing as deeply and as evenly as I could through the pain.

If I were not here, I would be dead. Jerzy's voice echoed in my mind from long ago, one of the first conversations we'd had. *I owe InterWorld my life.*

That was true for me, too. I'd Walked by accident the first time, and had drawn the attention of HEX. They'd sent people after me, and if not for Jay, I would have been captured and killed. I would have been one of those little blue lights used to power Joaquim.

You will not be able to Walk far enough away, Lord Dogknife had said.

Still breathing deeply, I cast out for a portal. The paralyzing, mind-numbing terror I felt at the thought that I wouldn't find one was replaced an instant later by relief strong enough to make my knees weak.

I couldn't get back to InterWorld, but I could still Walk. I could still sense portals. I could still move between worlds. I could find more of us.

I squared my shoulders, training taking over as I continued to move despite my injuries. I wouldn't let a few broken bones stop me, not now. I had things to do. I had the will, and a way, and more—far away from here and now, I had a ship.

And I could Walk farther than Lord Dogknife had ever dreamed.

Have you read Book 1?

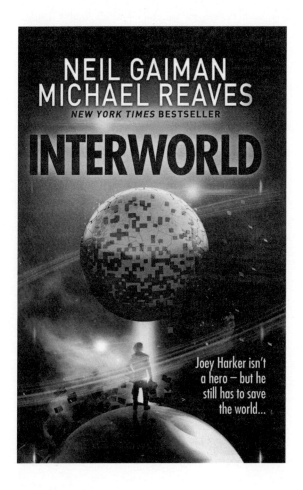

Joey's adventures to be continued in 2015!

NEIL GAIMAN was awarded the Newbery and Carnegie Medals for *The Graveyard Book*. His other books for younger readers include *Coraline* (which was made into an Academy Award–nominated film) and *The Day I Swapped My Dad for Two Goldfish* (which wasn't). Born in England, he has won both the Hugo and Nebula Awards. You can learn more at www.mousecircus.com.

MICHAEL REAVES is an Emmy Award–winning television writer, screenwriter, and novelist who has published many books, including the *New York Times* bestseller *Star Wars: Darth Maul: Shadow Hunter*. He's won a Howie Award and been nominated for both the Hugo and Nebula Awards. He lives in California.

MALLORY REAVES is best known for her adaptations of the popular manga series After School Nightmare, which was nominated for a 2007 Will Eisner Award. She lives in Riverside, California, with six cats, several friends, a dog, a snake, and a fish.